Uninvited Ghosts

HEDGEWITCH FOR HIRE – BOOK 7

CHRISTINE POPE

UNINVITED GHOSTS

Copyright © 2022 by Christine Pope

ISBN: 978-1-946435-53-8

Published by Dark Valentine Press

Cover design by Lou Harper

Ebook formatting by Indie Author Services

A Great Fall

"I CANNOT *BELIEVE* THIS HAPPENED!" JOSIE exclaimed, annoyed fingers clutching the thin hospital blanket that covered her. "I've been up and down those stairs literally *thousands* of times! And barely two weeks before your wedding!"

"It's okay," I assured her, even as I wondered whether everything truly was going to be okay. As the big day—June fourth—crept closer and closer, I'd come to rely on Josie more and more, since I had absolutely no experience planning an event of this scale. What I'd originally envisioned as a small, intimate ceremony with only Calvin's and my closest relations and our dearest friends in Globe had somehow ballooned into an extravagant event with a guest list of two hundred people and multiple entertainment/social areas plotted out on the grounds of the Bigelow mansion, the enormous Victorian house my mother and her husband Tom had bought almost a year earlier.

That Josie had just suffered a bad spill on her back steps and broken her ankle while taking out the trash seemed like a very bad omen, even though I generally did my best not to allow the normal ups and downs of life to acquire too much significance…cosmically speaking, anyway.

But no one could deny that losing my best helper with the wedding happening so soon was going to be tough on everyone involved. Josie would fret that she'd let me down, and Hazel Marr, my best friend and maid-of-honor, would be sure to think she'd have to pick up the slack. Hazel had even less experience than I did when it came to planning something as complicated as a wedding and reception for two hundred guests, and I knew she was already mildly freaking out. I'd told her that I could manage, that I didn't expect her to do anything more than what she'd already planned—namely, a girls' spa day the Thursday before the wedding, as well as the rehearsal dinner on Friday night—but I could tell she thought she'd have to shoulder the entire burden Josie had been cheerfully carrying all this time.

Josie made the same imperious hand wave I'd come to know and love, although it had slightly less impact from someone lying in a hospital bed.

At the best of times, she wasn't what you'd call a person of stature, since she barely touched five foot two, and yet when she was up and around, she had such a whirlwind of energy around her at all times that I hardly noticed how short she really was. Now, though, lying on her back and with only a touch of pink on her lips—I had a feeling Josie Woodrow would have to be in a coma before she'd allow herself to be seen with absolutely no makeup on—and her short-cropped copper-red hair distinctly mussed, she looked much more diminished than I'd expected.

"No, it is *not* okay," she declared, and shifted impatiently in her bed, almost as if she planned to push herself out of there by sheer force of will. However, she seemed to realize that injuring her ankle even further would only result in more hospital time, and so she settled against the pillows with an exasperated sigh. "The orthopedist says I should be released tomorrow, but he told me I absolutely have to stay off my foot for the next week, and after that, I can try crutches. In the meantime, he's sending me home in a wheel-chair. A *wheelchair!*" she added for extra empha-sis, as if I hadn't caught the word the first time.

"You'll do fine," I said. "I heard that Brett is making you ramps for the front and back stairs, right?"

At the mention of her nephew, who was

Globe's best and most in-demand contractor—and someone who'd saved my bacon the summer before when I discovered the true culprit behind the supposed demon infestation at the Bigelow mansion—Josie seemed to relax just a little bit.

"Yes, he's been very helpful. And thank goodness my bedroom is on the first floor of the house. If not, I'd be sleeping on the couch!"

"Well, now you don't have to worry about any of that," I said, my tone soothing. "And you don't have to worry about the wedding, either. All Calvin and I want is for you to get better—and to see you there, crutches or no."

"Wild horses wouldn't keep me away," she replied.

I could believe that. In a cage match between Josie Woodrow and a wild stallion, I'd put my money on Josie, even with crutches.

"Besides," I went on, "most of the heavy lifting is already done. All the vendors are in place, and everything's going smoothly. Hazel and I can manage it."

One of Josie's eyebrows went shooting up. They might not have been colored in with their usual auburn pencil, but they were just as emphatic nonetheless.

"Hazel is an admirable person," she said. "But wonderful as she is, I have a hard time believing she can manage all this on her own."

I had my own reservations, but I certainly wasn't going to voice them now. Josie needed to concentrate on healing and nothing else. "Hazel's not doing it on her own," I said smoothly. "We're working on everything together, and Jennifer Espinoza and Terry said they'd help out as well."

Jennifer was a local woman I'd become friends with while investigating the death of Danny Ortega, the former principal of Globe's one and only high school. Terry Woodrow was Josie's niece-in-law, and a total sweetheart. My complement of bridesmaids was rounded out by Madison Jeffers, my stepfather Tom's daughter, and his daughter-in-law Staci. I hadn't wanted to include either one of them in the wedding party, since we weren't at all close, but my mother had suggested it would be a good way to make Tom's family members feel included.

Right. Since Madison and Staci both lived five hundred miles away in Pacific Palisades, they weren't exactly available to help me with the wedding. In fact, Madison's sole contribution had been complaining that the bridesmaid's dresses I'd selected were too expensive—a statement I found kind of rich, considering her father opened his wallet pretty much whenever she put out her hand, and so I guessed she hadn't paid for the dress at all.

Anyway, I knew I couldn't rely on Madison—

or her sister-in-law—for much of anything except showing up just in time to go out with the rest of us bridesmaids, since I was footing the bill for that particular expedition. Actually, I was paying for pretty much the whole wedding myself, against the objections of Calvin's parents, who'd wanted to pitch in. But I'd told them I could manage just fine, and the only thing I wanted was for them to come to the wedding and have a wonderful time. Luckily, since I'd finally managed to win them over despite not being part of the shapeshifter-coyote San Ramon Apache tribe, I knew they'd be able to enjoy the day without reservations.

Assuming the whole thing didn't collapse into disaster now that Josie wouldn't be able to bring us over the finish line.

Because Josie couldn't exactly turn up her nose at the help being offered by her niece-in-law or the other locals involved in the wedding, she had to settle for releasing a dramatic sigh. "I certainly hope so," she said. "But I still can't help but worry."

"Well, don't," I told her. "Worrying isn't good for your health. I can manage just fine, even if it means closing down the store for the next two weeks so I have enough time to handle everything."

Her eyes flared with alarm. "Oh, you can't do that!"

"Really, it's no big deal," I said, which was nothing more than the truth. Once in a Blue Moon was the pretty little New Age store I owned and operated in the heart of Globe's tiny downtown, and the place had proved to be more popular than one might have expected. Still, the town wasn't going to collapse if people couldn't buy incense or Tarot cards for the next two weeks. "Or," I added hastily, since I could tell Josie was still looking worried and dubious, "I'll just open for limited hours, like afternoons only or whatever. I'll figure it out."

Luckily, I didn't have to depend on the income from the store to support myself. The shop was definitely self-sustaining, but the vast majority of my wealth had come via an unexpected inheritance from Lucien Dumond, former head of the Greater Los Angeles Necromancers' Guild. Even though I'd given what felt like gobs of money away to various charities during the intervening time, the money still seemed to keep growing, thanks to the way I'd socked chunks of it away in various investments recommended by my stepfather Tom's financial advisor. At the rate I was going, I could probably close the store and never work again and still not know what to do with all of it.

Josie seemed somewhat mollified by that

compromise, because she didn't argue but only said, "Well, if you think it's necessary—"

"It might not be," I said. "I'm just saying it's an option if it comes to that. I'd planned to close everything down after next Tuesday anyway."

Because even I had realized that working up until the very last minute probably wasn't a very good idea, and so I'd had signs in my window for weeks saying that Once in a Blue Moon would be closed from Wednesday, June first, through Monday, June thirteenth. Although my visions of a honeymoon in New Orleans hadn't materialized—Calvin had rightly pointed out that going in early June would result in a hot and sticky trip—we were instead heading to California for a leisurely wander through Napa and Sonoma, and would be gone for more than a week.

"Oh, true," Josie replied. She fidgeted with a fold of the crocheted afghan that covered her— the work of her niece-in-law Terry, I guessed, since I knew she was crafty and made lots of things like that, and probably had dropped it off so Josie would be more comfortable during her hospital stay. "I suppose that makes it a little better." She paused there, then added, "If I do get to go home tomorrow, do you think you could swing by in the afternoon? There are some things we should probably go over about the wedding if you and Hazel really are going to be handling everything."

"Sure," I said at once. "I'm not sure if Hazel can make it, because I know she has an appointment with a gallery manager in Gilbert, but—"

"Just you is fine," Josie said hastily. "Anything Hazel needs to know, you can pass along to her."

"Sounds like a plan." I'd been sitting on a chair next to Josie's bedside during this entire conversation, but I rose then, figuring we'd said everything that needed to be said. And it wasn't as though I had to worry about leaving her alone, because I knew that Joyce Lewis, the police chief's wife and someone I'd become friendly with, had told me she planned to stop by and see Josie sometime that afternoon as well.

And no doubt someone else would arrive to take her place, ensuring that Josie would have company all the way until visiting hours ended. The small private room was filled with floral arrangements in a dizzying array of colors and shapes and sizes, flowery proof of Josie's popularity in the community.

"I'll call you," she promised, and I smiled.

"Looking forward to it. Take care—and rest."

"I will," she promised.

Whether she'd keep that promise was another story. Josie was such a force of nature, I had a hard time envisioning her meekly sitting in a chair for the next week, covered in one of Terry's afghans and waiting for her broken ankle to heal.

But that was between Josie and her orthopedist. I gave her another smile, then headed out.

"You honestly think you can manage an entire wedding and reception by yourself?" Archie asked, his tone pure skepticism. "You haven't even been able to turn me back into a man."

Here we go again, I thought, but obviously, I didn't bother to say anything out loud. The cursed cat who'd been my companion ever since I moved to Globe more than a year earlier still couldn't resist needling me about his continued feline state, and by that point, I'd vowed to let it all roll off my back.

Some days I was more successful at that than others.

And really, I had tried. I'd ordered arcane spell books from all over the globe, had concocted potions that smelled foul and tasted even worse. I'd cast spells and uttered charms, had performed every single ritual I thought might be of some help, including a particularly ridiculous one where I'd donned a pair of cat ears and drunk an extremely foul-tasting cup of catnip tea.

Absolutely none of it had worked. Archie was

still the same big smoke-gray cat I'd let in from the balcony all those months earlier. Although I hadn't quite given up hope, I'd definitely resigned myself to the sad fact that he wouldn't be able to attend the wedding in human form as I'd promised him just a few months earlier.

Not that Archie was terribly keen to attend Calvin's and my nuptials. He'd grudgingly accepted Calvin's presence in my life, and even more grudgingly agreed to come live with us in Calvin's lovely pueblo-style house out on the San Ramon Apache reservation, but that was more because he didn't have any other options than because he was looking forward to cohabiting with a newly married couple. It wasn't jealousy; Archie had told me on our first meeting he was asexual and not interested in a romantic relationship with anyone. No, it was more that, as someone with a whole mess of Virgo aspects in his chart, he had some major problems with change.

And some *very* big changes were coming.

"No, I haven't been able to change you back," I said mildly. "And I'm really sorry about that. But I think we can all agree that managing a wedding is a lot different from casting a successful spell… especially one as complicated and delicate as unraveling a seventy-year-old curse."

Archie's ears flattened against his head after that remark. Although he didn't appear to have aged a day since the time an unknown witch had hurled a curse at him back in the early 1950s, he still hated to be reminded of how much time he'd spent in his feline state.

"Not being a witch," he said, his tone acid, "I can't comment on that. But a wedding has a huge amount of moving parts, and you've never done anything like this before."

"And what do *you* know about weddings?" I inquired. By that point, I'd gone into the kitchen to brew myself some tea. Yes, it was almost ninety degrees outside, but sometimes you just wanted a nice cup of Darjeeling.

Maybe my nerves were more jangled than I'd thought.

Archie bristled, his tail whipping back and forth. "More than you might think," he retorted.

I almost inquired why an asexual man would care anything about weddings, and decided it wasn't worth the resulting drama. "Really?" I asked as I put the kettle on the stove and turned on the gas.

"Really," Archie replied. "I've seen quite a few of those shows on the television."

More than once, I'd wondered what Archie did all day while I was at work…or while I was away at Calvin's house. On a couple of occasions, I'd suspected that he'd been watching TV, since the remote looked as though it had been moved and it didn't always land on the same streaming service when I turned my Apple TV back on. However, when I'd asked Archie about it, he'd been vociferous in his denials, saying he had better things to do than melt his brain cells while watching television.

Methinks the cat doth protest too much, I thought then, doing my best to hold back a grin.

"So…you watch reality television?" I asked.

"On very rare occasions," he said, now looking as though he wished he'd kept his mouth shut. "But I do think the shows about weddings are interesting. So much planning, so many small details to keep track of."

Well, I had to admit that sort of thing might appeal to someone with a Virgo stellium—that is, someone with more than three planets in one sign. Archie was very good at the small stuff, a quality which grated on my nerves from time to time but would probably be an admirable quality in a wedding planner. I'd often wondered whether Josie had a lot of Virgo or possibly Capricorn placements, since she was equally good at fussing over details, but she would never let me do her chart.

"I prefer to be a woman of mystery," she'd told me, and I had to be content to leave it at that.

"Anyway," Archie went on as I got my favorite hand-painted mug out of the cupboard, "since you've never done anything like this before, and because you sometimes do let the small things slip your notice, I'm not sure whether you know exactly what you're taking on. Or Hazel," he added darkly when I opened my mouth to protest that I wasn't going to be doing everything myself.

Well, my cursed cat had a point there. I loved Hazel to death, but she did tend to let her artistic nature take over when she was working on a new piece, and sometimes neglected the day-to-day. Chuck Langdon, her fiancé—the couple had gotten engaged at the beginning of May—was much more the practical type, and I could tell he didn't mind the way her head tended to get stuck in the clouds when she was really involved in a painting. No, he just loved her because of her enormous talent and her warm heart, which was as it should be.

However, Archie was probably right. The two of us were not exactly the people you'd choose to run your wedding. I wasn't an artist like Hazel, but I did tend to have more of a macro than a micro view of things.

Unfortunately, I didn't have much choice in this particular case. And, as I'd told Josie, a lot of the heavy lifting had already been handled. All I had to do was keep steering this ship in the same direction it had been pointed, and everything should work out just fine.

"We'll be okay," I said. "And I know Calvin will pitch in as well."

Archie made a noncommittal sound, probably because he knew as well as I did that Calvin's job was a lot more demanding than mine, and there was never any way to know when he might be called to the scene of a crime or to manage a domestic dispute.

Or to get someone's marauding cows off tribal land, a problem that seemed to occur more often than any other local crises I could think of. He'd managed to wrangle a precious ten days off for our honeymoon, but I also knew Calvin couldn't drop everything and come running every time I had a problem with the caterers or discovered that the wrong shade of chair covers had been delivered.

Well, I wouldn't sweat it. A few bobbles wouldn't ruin the wedding, after all, and might just provide some fodder for jokes down the line. The more I stressed about every single little detail, the more chance I'd drive myself crazy and not be able to enjoy this very special day, which was the most important thing.

Everything would work out just fine in the end.

2

Planned Obsolescence

BECAUSE CALVIN WAS WORKING LATE THAT night, I had a quiet evening with Archie. In fact, I even turned on a wedding planner reality show, thinking I might as well try to get an insider's view of what I could expect to deal with over the course of the next few weeks. However, since this was reality television, every little issue or problem that cropped up was treated like a crisis of the first order, rather than the sort of thing that could get shrugged off in service to the greater good.

But having the show on appeared to mollify Archie, who still seemed extra-cranky about remaining a cat even though the wedding was looming ever nearer, and I thought it was time well spent. All the same, I went to bed earlier than I normally would, figuring with everything I had on my plate, the extra sleep would do me good.

The next day, things were slow enough at the store that I was more than a little relieved when Josie called shortly after three. Hearing from her always helped to break up the monotony.

"I know you're still working," she said. "But is there any chance you could come over to my house now?"

"Absolutely," I said at once. My last customer had walked through the door more than two hours earlier, and I had no reason to believe anyone else would be showing up any time soon. Early summer was almost always quiet; spring and fall were spectacular times of year to visit the region because the weather in central Arizona was so accommodating, but even in Globe, things could start to get pretty toasty around the end of May and the beginning of June. So far, we'd touched the nineties but hadn't swung all the way into them, and I kept praying things would stay that way until after the wedding. I knew the ceremony would be beautiful no matter what, and yet I still didn't want to be dripping with sweat the entire time.

So I put the little "be back at" sign in the window, indicating the store would remain closed until ten o'clock the next morning, then locked up and headed out back to where my little Denim Edition Volkswagen Beetle convertible was parked behind the building. The sun blazed down from overhead, but because Brett Woodrow had erected one of those portable aluminum carports for me directly behind the building, the car wasn't as hot as it might otherwise have been.

To be honest, I probably could have walked to Josie's house. However, since the day was warm and her home was about a half mile uphill from my store, it seemed smarter to drive. I didn't want to risk getting overheated—or worse, get sunburned—with the wedding only ten days away.

When I got to her place, I noticed immediately that there was a shiny red Mercedes SUV parked in the driveway. Since Josie drove a Lincoln, I knew the vehicle couldn't be hers. And although I couldn't profess to have every single car in Globe memorized, the Mercedes GLS was definitely memorable enough that I knew I'd never seen it before.

A visiting nurse? Maybe, but if that was the case, the field was more lucrative than I'd thought.

Frowning a little, I slung my purse over my shoulder and got out of my car. Even with sunglasses protecting my eyes, the day felt almost ominously bright, and I hoped we might get a little cloud cover on the day of the wedding itself. Not a full-blown monsoon storm—although it was early in the year for that sort of thing—but just a few high clouds to block some light and heat.

When I rang the bell, the brick-red front door opened almost immediately. Standing there was a woman I knew I'd never seen before, probably in her early thirties like me. Unlike me, however, she was almost ethereally blonde, with pale hair lying in smooth ripples over her shoulders, porcelain-pale skin, and blue eyes brighter than my own soft gray-blue.

Blinking at the stranger, I said, "Um…I'm here to see Josie?"

The sentence ended on an upward inflection, making it sound as though I was asking a question. Actually, I supposed I was, although the real question involved this stranger's identity and not this visit to see my friend.

The vision smiled—showing teeth so perfect, they looked like they should be in a toothpaste commercial—and said, "Oh, you must be the bride. I'm Victoria Parrish. Come on in."

She stepped aside so I could enter the house, and I went in, feeling more mystified than ever. Victoria Parrish was wearing a chic sleeveless sheath dress in a soft French blue that perfectly complemented her angelic coloring, and so I doubted she was a visiting nurse or someone from the hospital. Those high-heeled sling-back sandals she had on didn't look very practical.

A relative of Josie's who'd come to help out? Maybe, but if that was the case, I didn't see much of a family resemblance. And again, Victoria didn't look as though she was dressed to help someone in and out of a wheelchair or do a few chores around the house.

She led me into the living room, where Josie was sitting on the sofa, her feet up on the cushion, her legs covered by an afghan even though the weather certainly didn't call for one. I guessed the afghan was probably an attempt to hide the bulky cast on her right leg. Cool air blew through the vents above us, and so at least she didn't have to worry about getting too overheated.

"Oh, Selena," she said as soon as I entered with my unexpected guide. "Go ahead and sit down. I see you've already met Victoria."

"Yes," I replied politely, then took a seat in one of the wing chairs opposite the couch where Josie was reclining. I noticed that a pitcher of iced tea and a plate of iced lemon bars from Cloud Coffee sat on the coffee table, along with three glasses and some nicely arranged paper napkins and matching floral paper plates. The whole scene made me feel as though I'd been invited to a tea party I didn't even know about, and my sense of mystification only increased.

During this exchange, Victoria had seated herself in the other wing chair. She offered me an apologetic smile and said, "Josie told me about the situation—I'm only too happy to help."

"'Situation'?" I repeated, shooting an inquiring glance in Josie's direction.

"I just couldn't bear the thought of you having to manage all this on your own," she said breezily. "And so I called Victoria for help. She's a wedding planner."

Oh, boy. Because I'd had Josie on my side, I hadn't even considered hiring a planner to help out with the wedding. To be perfectly honest, I'd always had a bit of a mental struggle with the concept of inviting a complete stranger to get involved with what was supposed to be one of the most important and emotionally intimate moments in a person's life. No, I'd never been one of those women who believed her wedding day was the be-all and end-all of existence, but....

"I know this must come as something of a surprise," Victoria said. She still had that air of apology around her, and so I couldn't really get too irritated by her presence here. After all, she was only responding to Josie's call for help. "But a wedding and reception for two hundred guests is a lot for anyone to handle. I just want your day to be worry-free so you can relax and enjoy it."

"And I appreciate that," I replied, leaning over so I could grab a glass and pour myself some iced tea. My mouth was way too dry; I hated confrontations.

Not that this little meeting had devolved into anything remotely resembling a confrontation, but still, I couldn't help being upset at Josie for putting me in this position.

She must have noted some kind of shift in my expression, because my friend said hastily, "I know I blindsided you with this, Selena, but Victoria's right. You need to be able to relax and enjoy your day, and not be trying to put out fires the whole time. And there will be fires," she added, as I opened my mouth to tell her there shouldn't be any fires, that we'd already taken care of all the little fiddly bits and everything should go smoothly. "You know what they say—no plan survives a battlefield."

"Are you referring to my wedding reception as a battlefield?" I inquired, although I couldn't help smiling a bit at that description.

"Of course not," Victoria put in. She was also smiling a little, but in a friendly way, as though she completely understood where I was coming from. "But when you have that many moving parts, there's always something that crops up, no matter how careful you've been. Do you really want to be off supervising the caterer instead of sipping champagne and chatting with your guests?"

She had a point there. And I recalled all too clearly the dust-up at Josie's Halloween party when the caterer misread her instructions and brought crab dip instead of the shrimp platter she'd ordered. The mishap had been brushed aside, overshadowed by the far bigger issue of poor Danny Ortega dropping dead in the middle of the shindig, but I had no doubt Josie would never hire that caterer again.

Did I really want to hover around the caterer, making sure they'd brought brie instead of camembert, or whatever other minor mix-up might occur?

Josie correctly interpreted my silence as a signal that I was beginning to budge, because she put in, "Victoria has planned hundreds of weddings. Why, she's one of the most in-demand wedding planners in Scottsdale! The only reason she's available now is because the wedding she was planning for June fourth was canceled abruptly after the bride caught her groom cheating with one of the bridesmaids."

Ouch. Thank the Goddess, I didn't have to worry about that kind of behavior with Calvin. He loved me with his whole heart, and was as honest as the day was long. No way in the world would he cheat on me. If he ever fell out of love—something I really couldn't see happening—I knew he would be honest with me about it.

Those gloomy thoughts were not the sort of thing I wanted to be pondering with only ten days remaining until my own ceremony, and so I pushed them out of the way, saying, "I'm sorry to hear that."

Victoria's shoulders lifted. She had just the faintest hint of tan, warm against the soft blue of the dress she was wearing. If it had been sprayed on, it was very subtle, just enough to give her a summery sort of glow. "It happens every once in a while. Not too often with my own clients, because I try to be picky about who I work with. A lot of the time, I can tell whose relationship is going to last and who's going to be filing for divorce within the year."

Was she psychic?

No, that guess didn't feel quite right to me, although it wasn't as if I had some sort of secret talent for sniffing out other psychics. I had a feeling it was more that she'd worked with a lot of people, and simply had good instincts.

"Anyway," Josie went on, "I reached out to Victoria mostly because I was looking for a recommendation—I'd never expected she would be available on such short notice—but then she told me about her cancellation, and the whole thing just feels like fate to me."

Maybe it was. I certainly didn't want to think the hand of fate was what had pushed Josie down the back stairs of her house, but after she'd suffered that unfortunate fall, possibly the universe was doing what it could to ensure Calvin's and my big day would be as hassle-free as possible.

Victoria smiled. "I don't know about fate, but I'm certainly happy to help."

Both women were gazing at me, clearly expecting some sort of reply. And although I had to admit I had a stubborn streak I'd never been quite able to overcome, I also wanted to think I'd evolved enough in my almost thirty-one years on the planet to realize it was okay to accept help when it was offered, especially when it involved an event that was so important to me. After all, I'd accepted Josie's offer of assistance way back in December when she first learned about my engagement. What would be the point in turning Victoria down now, except to prove I wasn't quite as evolved as I liked to think?

"And I'm very glad to accept your help," I said. "But I'll take care of your fee."

Because of course I knew that Josie had already planned to cover the cost of hiring a wedding planner, driven by guilt over being knocked out of commission...even if none of it was her fault.

Victoria shot Josie an uncertain look. "That's very kind, Selena, but—"

"But I'm already taking care of it," Josie broke in. "If I hadn't been so ridiculously clumsy, we wouldn't be in this mess."

Still holding my glass of iced tea, I settled against the back of my wing chair. "Josie, none of this is your fault. I certainly don't expect you to pay for my wedding planner." I paused there, and fixed her with a direct stare I hoped she could tell meant business. "And if you won't let me pay, then I'm afraid I can't accept Victoria's services."

The two women traded a glance, Victoria's almost embarrassed, as if she really didn't care for such open talk about money, while Josie's bright blue gaze was determined. I knew she didn't like me trying to dictate the terms of our little agreement, but no way was I going to let her pay what I guessed must be some fairly hefty fees.

However, after a long, tense moment, she apparently decided it was better to let me foot the bill than have me try to manage all the logistics of the ceremony and the reception on my own. "All right," she said, her tone just bordering on ungracious…but not enough to make the scene any more uncomfortable than it already was.

"It would be lower than my usual fee," Victoria put in. While I couldn't say she looked exactly relieved, she did seem a little less tense now that it appeared as though Josie wasn't going to offer any more arguments. "Considering you and Josie have already done so much work."

"That's fine," I said. Really, money wasn't the issue, but no point in explaining to her that I was sitting on a large inheritance I still wasn't sure I should have gotten in the first place.

"Great," she replied. Now she did look relaxed, and even leaned forward to get herself a glass of iced tea so she could take a sip. After she was done with that, she added, "Do you think we could meet tomorrow afternoon sometime? I want to go over all your plans and get a copy of everything so I can take over right away."

I wasn't sure I really liked the phrase "take over," but I supposed that was exactly what Victoria would be doing—picking up the reins so I could focus on the important stuff...including not looking like a frazzled wreck by the time my wedding day swung around. Calvin loved me no matter what, but I wanted to make sure I was a beautiful blooming bride for him.

"Sure," I said, but then went on, "Isn't that going to be a lot of driving for you?"

"Oh, no worries," Josie cut in, now almost beaming. Maybe she was happy that she'd gotten her way, and was willing to brush aside the issue of who was paying the wedding planner she'd found. "Victoria's going to be staying in one of

Mavis's Airbnbs until the Monday after the wedding."

One would think that paying for one of Josie's friend's vacation rentals would eat substantially into Victoria's fees, but if I knew Josie, she'd already negotiated a special rate…or was paying for the whole thing herself. Maybe that was why she hadn't put up more of a fight about covering the cost of hiring a wedding planner.

And although I supposed I could have tried to continue the argument, I decided it wasn't worth it, if for no other reason than it didn't make a lot of sense to have Victoria driving a good hour and a half or more each way every time she needed to come out to Globe and handle something.

"Oh, well," I said. "Then let's say…four o'clock tomorrow?"

That meant I'd be closing the shop an hour early, but if the foot traffic I'd been getting lately was any indication, it wouldn't matter very much.

"Perfect," Victoria replied. "Then I'll meet you at your apartment tomorrow at four."

I didn't bother to ask her if she had the address. Clearly, Josie had already filled her in on all the pertinent details. I smiled, and we chatted a little about Globe and about the weather, and then I headed out.

Good thing Calvin and I already had plans to barbecue at his place that night.

We had a lot to talk about.

To my relief, he seemed more amused by the concept of having a wedding planner than anything else. "Looks like Hurricane Josie has struck again," he remarked, then took a sip of malbec.

We were sitting out on his patio, enjoying the warm late afternoon sun as he grilled tri-tip, his specialty. I could have made remarks about having a heavy meal when I needed to fit into my wedding gown in less than two weeks, but I let it slide. While the dress was beautiful, I'd made sure not to get something so form-fitting that I'd have to diet for a month just to squeeze into it. We had so much wonderful food planned for the reception that I wanted to make sure I could happily eat what I wanted without stressing about it too much.

"Yes," I replied. "Although in this case, I'm happy for her interference. I suppose Hazel and I could have managed somehow, but it's kind of nice to know that we really don't have to try."

"Our mothers could have pitched in," Calvin said. He eyeballed the tri-tip, then picked up his barbecue tongs and flipped the chunk of meat over, sending up a toothsome-smelling sizzle from the flames beneath. "It's not like my mother hasn't helped out with a ton of weddings."

That was probably no more than the truth, considering Calvin was one of five siblings and had an absolutely enormous extended family. Still….

"I know," I said. "But I also want our parents to be able to enjoy themselves and not be running around with their hair on fire. Also, my mother won't even be getting here until the middle of next week."

Which reminded me that I needed to head over to the mansion and take a look around, make sure everything was ready for hers and Tom's arrival. They had a gardener who came by every week to keep the grounds in tip-top shape, and an occasional housekeeper who'd scrub the place from top to bottom after every visit by vacation renters, but still, I knew I'd feel better if I went through the entire house just to reassure myself it was ready for an extended visit from its owners. The plan was for them to arrive the Wednesday before the ceremony and then head out the Monday afterward, which would be the longest they'd ever stayed in the house.

Calvin shrugged. "Just thought I'd offer."

I got up from my chair and went over to the grill so I could give him a hug. "And I really appreciate it," I told him. "But I think it'll be better to let Victoria handle things. She's a professional, and I'm sure there isn't a wedding curveball she hasn't seen already."

His eyebrows lifted slightly. "You like her?"

"Well, it was a pretty brief meeting," I replied. "But yes, I got a good vibe off her. She just wants to ensure we have the best day possible."

"I'll drink to that," Calvin said, and raised his glass.

I dutifully clinked mine against his and took a swallow of malbec. With the rich wine on my tongue and the warm sun against my hair, I experienced a moment of utter well-being. Yes, this was exactly where I was supposed to be.

And with Victoria handling all the minutiae, I knew I could relax and just let time roll on until our big day.

Everything was going to be fine.

3

Blight Spirit

I STAYED AT CALVIN'S HOUSE THAT NIGHT, since he didn't have to be at work until nine and I'd made sure to leave out plenty of food for Archie. Still, the cursed cat really hated it when I waltzed in right before the store was due to open and didn't spend any time at all with him, so I left a little after eight-thirty and drove over to the apartment with the sun at my back. Oddly, the flat above the shop was already beginning to feel not like my home anymore. True, I'd spent a lot of time at Calvin's place lately, but I didn't think that was entirely it. No, I guessed it was more that I knew I wouldn't be living here after we returned from our wine country honeymoon.

Not that you'd know from looking at the apartment. I'd already made the decision not to worry about boxing up any of my stuff and taking it over to the house Calvin and I would soon share until after we got back from California. He'd cleared out the third bedroom, which he'd been using mostly for storage, so I could set it up as my office and meditation space once we were cohabiting, but it sat empty for now. Maybe I was being superstitious, but something deep within had told me not to take down my altar and all the good energy it had been accumulating over the past year until after the wedding and honeymoon were both safely in the past.

Archie was lying in a patch of sun by the window when I came in, although he cracked an eyelid as soon as I closed the door. "Nice of you to drop by."

"You could always come over to Calvin's house with me," I said sweetly, and the cat gave an irritated shake of his head.

"No, thanks," he replied. "I prefer to put off the evil day for as long as possible."

Since we'd been back and forth on the topic multiple times, I decided to let it go. He was coming with me to Calvin's house just as soon as we got back from our honeymoon—Hazel had offered to watch Archie while we were away, something Chuck wasn't too thrilled about—and nothing in the world was going to change that eventual outcome.

Well, unless a miracle occurred and I

somehow managed to break the curse that had kept Archie a cat for the past seventy years, something neither one of us was really counting on at this point.

"Suit yourself," I replied. Then, because I knew Archie hated disruptions to his routine and needed advance notice of any deviations from the norm, I went on, "Oh, I'm having a visitor this afternoon. Josie broke her ankle and can't really help out with the wedding, so we hired a wedding planner to take over. She's coming by late this afternoon."

Archie wrinkled his nose. "You couldn't meet her at Calvin's house?"

"No," I said severely. "She wanted to come here. I can't expect her to drive all the way out there—I don't even know if her SUV has four-wheel drive."

"*Your* car doesn't," the cat pointed out.

True enough, but even though I was willing to batter my little convertible's suspension every time I drove over to Calvin's place, that didn't mean I expected Victoria Parrish to do the same. "She's staying at one of Mavis Jones' Airbnbs here in Globe," I said coolly. "It just makes more sense to meet here at the apartment."

Archie looked as though he was trying to come up with about fifty more arguments as to why I shouldn't have a visitor, but something in my expression must have told him it would be a waste of time.

"Fine," he replied. "I suppose I shall just have to hide out in the office."

Considering that was where his bed was located, I didn't think he was making much of a sacrifice. But whatever. If he wanted to skulk in my office rather than be anywhere near Victoria Parrish, I was just fine with that. This meeting wasn't about him, after all.

"Oh," I continued, trying not to be inwardly amused by the look of annoyance that passed over his feline features when he realized I wasn't finished with him, "and I'm going to head out to the Bigelow house during lunch to take a quick look at things. I'll feed you before I go."

"Try not to over-exert yourself," he grumped, and then stalked off down the hallway.

By that point I was pretty much used to those sorts of reactions. He also hated it when I ran errands during my lunch break, since he seemed to believe spending time outside the apartment meant he was last on my list of priorities. That wasn't even remotely the truth, but at the same time, I had a life to live. I couldn't spend every waking moment catering to a cursed cat's needs, even if he did seem to believe he should be the center of my universe.

At least I'd done my duty and informed him

of the day's plans. There wasn't much else I could do beyond that.

Well, besides turn him back into a man, and since it seemed more likely that I'd win the lottery a second time than discover the key to breaking that particularly nasty spell, I wasn't going to hold my breath.

I called out, "Heading downstairs!" and then took my purse and went down to the store to get it ready for the start of business hours at ten o'clock. Maybe no one would even come in to shop, but it wouldn't be because I'd dropped the ball.

***

Since it was extremely slow that morning, I cheated and closed for lunch about ten minutes early so I could run over to Cloud Coffee and pick up a sandwich and some iced green tea for my trip over to the Bigelow mansion. That way, I wouldn't have to worry about finding the time to scrounge something at home after I was done with my errand.

Just like the day before, the sky overhead was an absolutely perfect blue, uncluttered by even a single cloud. It was also almost uncomfortably warm, so, as beautiful as the weather looked to the eye, I had to hope once again that things would be a little cooler on the day of the ceremony. We were going to have several large pavilions set up on the grounds, and those pavilions were equipped with little misting devices to keep things somewhat comfortable, but still, I couldn't help worrying that we were going to have at least one guest collapse from heat exhaustion before the day was over.

Maybe we should have moved the wedding to early autumn, when the weather would be better.

But it was too late to worry about that now... and besides, I knew I couldn't possibly have waited that long to become Calvin's wife.

I pulled up in front of the large four-bay garage that sat a little ways from the house itself and turned off the ignition, then got out. A warm breeze caught at my hair, although it felt almost playful, as if assuring me that as long as we had a little wind the day of the wedding, the June temperatures would feel just fine.

Smiling slightly, I made my way up the flag-stone walk, bordered on either side by some of the lushest and biggest roses I'd ever seen. They bloomed in shades of red and pink and yellow and bright apricot orange, and were part of the reason why I'd decided to have similarly colorful flowers for my bouquet and for the centerpieces at the reception. The style now was to have muted shades of white on white, but I knew such understated floral arrangements would be completely overshadowed by the Bigelow mansion's exuberant gardens.

Just before I began to mount the front steps, a flicker of movement at one of the upstairs windows caught my eye. I paused, then lowered my sunglasses slightly with the hand that wasn't holding the house keys. At once, the glare of the day made me blink. Damn, it was bright out here.

There it was again—just a flutter of movement, as if someone had been holding the curtain aside and then let go as soon as they noticed me looking up at them.

That was impossible, though. The house was completely empty; the last people to stay here had been a family from Colorado who'd rented the place for a week at the end of April. My mother had made sure to list the property on Airbnb as unavailable for all of May and June, since she didn't want to take the risk of anything happening to the house right when she and Tom were finally going to come for an extended stay.

Well, the sun was insanely bright today. I probably hadn't seen anything at all, or at least nothing more than a reflection from a bird flying by.

I went up the rest of the steps, then paused to open the door.

As soon as it swung inward, some cool air

flowed outward, telling me the central A/C was working just fine. It was probably foolish to leave it on all the time, but at least the temperature was set at seventy-five, and not the bone-chilling—to me, anyway—sixty-five degrees that my mother preferred.

A quick glance around told me everything seemed to be in order. The beautiful antique furniture that had come with the house was all where it was supposed to be, and all the dark wood surfaces gleamed. That surprised me a little; I would have expected things to be a little dusty, since no one had been in here for nearly a month and the housekeeper wasn't scheduled to come in until next Tuesday, right before my mother and Tom were due to arrive in Globe.

Well, the place had been closed up tight, so maybe it just hadn't gotten the opportunity to be dusty. I knew I should be glad the housekeeper wouldn't have to do that much to get the house ready.

And yet....

Something didn't feel right.

I couldn't say exactly what, because all I had to go on was that odd little glimpse of someone—some*thing*—at the upstairs window. That...and a creepy-crawly sensation all down the back of my neck, beginning to slide along my spine.

The sort of feeling I got when I entered a haunted house.

That was ridiculous, though. I'd been in this house plenty of times and had never gotten even the slightest hint there was any kind of otherworldly presence here. No, not even when the place had given every sign that it had been infested by demons.

Of course, those demons had been utterly fake, just a ruse cooked up by Miriam Jacobsen, the former head of the Globe Chamber of Commerce, and her lackey Al Loomis as a way to get my parents to sell the place cheap so she could turn around and make millions by selling the property to some investors who wanted to turn the gorgeous hilltop site into a resort. Still, despite the physical evidence of infestation—horrible sounds and smells, for the most part—I'd never gotten the same sort of chill I was feeling now.

My gaze moved toward the stairs. Even though I knew there were no demons here, I still disliked going up and down that grand staircase, since that was where paranormal investigator and part-time exorcist Brant Thoreau had met his untimely death. It wasn't demons who'd pushed him, but Al Loomis, who was now safely locked up in a maximum-security prison down the road in Florence, just like his employer Miriam. And while I knew Brant had moved on from this plane, I shivered a little every time I had to go up those stairs.

But...what if he hadn't moved on? What if his spirit still haunted this place?

No, that didn't make any sense. I'd been in and out of the house multiple times since then, and I hadn't once detected even a hint of his presence.

Then again, ghosts didn't always follow any sort of strict rules. Just because Brant hadn't been hanging around since the moment of his death didn't mean he might not have decided to return to the scene of the crime if he thought he had some unfinished business to handle.

The skin at the back of my neck prickled again, and I pulled in a deep breath. Unlike demons, ghosts weren't anything to be afraid of. If Brant still lingered here, then I needed to reach out and see what he wanted.

My hand stole into my purse and drew out the little lump of rough black tourmaline I carried in an inner pocket as a protection against negative energy and whatever bad juju might be floating around nearby. The stone felt cool against my fingers, telling me there wasn't anything evil in the immediate vicinity.

But just because I couldn't sense something bad didn't mean a ghost might not still be lingering here. On their own, ghosts weren't good or evil, only spirits trapped in this world because they were either fearful to move on to the next life or—like Danny Ortega, who'd hung around so he could discover who'd slipped that poison into his drink at Josie's Halloween party—they had some sort of business they needed to get settled before they felt comfortable sliding into the next phase of their existence.

Well, there was only one thing I could do.

Still clutching the piece of black tourmaline, I mounted the first set of steps and then paused on the landing so I could stand there quietly and let the energies of the house drift around me. The place felt utterly quiet, but at the same time, I still had a sensation of almost pressure, as if something was disturbing the atmosphere inside the mansion.

I didn't hear any spectral voices telling me to get out, though, and so I pulled in a breath, told myself to put on my big-girl psychic panties, and went up to the second floor, where all the home's bedrooms were located. The house had an enormous attic that occupied the entire third floor, but I sincerely hoped I wouldn't have to go up there. No, there wasn't anything terribly creepy about the attic, since it mostly housed cast-off furniture, boxes of Christmas ornaments, and the like, and yet I still didn't much enjoy the idea of prowling around in there by myself.

All the bedroom doors stood open, and I assured myself that was a good thing, since that would make it harder for anything to creep up on me. One by one, I looked inside each bedroom, and didn't see anything except a lot of lovingly decorated spaces, each with its own color and theme.

Even so, I kept the bedroom that looked out over the front yard for last.

But at length I couldn't put it off any longer. I peeked inside and saw it was a large space, nearly as big as the master suite, which occupied the opposite side of the second floor and overlooked the property's extensive gardens to the rear of the house. This room, however, hadn't been furnished as a bedroom, but had been set up as an office, with a set of really gorgeous antique barrister bookcases with glass fronts, and a big mahogany desk with matching file cabinets flanking it on either side. An enormous Persian rug in warm shades of rust and sage and tan covered the wood floor.

All in all, there wasn't anything in the room to start my alarms pinging, but at the same time, it was as though that sensation of pressure grew stronger here, as if there was something inside that really didn't want me to go any farther.

Probably, I should have taken that feeling as a sign to get the heck out of there. On the other hand, my mother and Tom would be getting here in less than a week, and the last thing I wanted was for them to have to contend with any unexpected visitors of the spectral kind.

Another deep breath to ground myself, and then I stepped into the office and said clearly, "Is there anyone here? My name is Selena. I'd like to help you, if that's all right."

No reply, of course, just a sort of silence that felt somehow sharper, as if whoever or whatever was here had suddenly focused all its attention on me.

Yikes.

I reminded myself that being timid wouldn't help me solve this particular mystery, so instead of turning around and bolting the way I would have liked to do, I instead stood in that same spot just inside the door.

"Is this your house?"

Again, nothing but silence.

The air around me grew colder, though, so much colder than it should have been, even with the A/C quietly working away in the background. I knew a temperature drop was a common phenomenon where ghosts were involved, but that didn't make my current situation any less uncomfortable.

I wished I had someone here with me—not just because I would have felt a lot better about communicating with some unknown ghost, but also because that way I'd have a witness to corroborate the phenomena I was experiencing.

"I don't mean you any harm," I went on, since I didn't quite know what else to say. I also had to wonder why this spirit was manifesting now, when my mother had been renting the place out as an Airbnb for the past six months and not a single person had reported seeing or hearing…or feeling…anything out of the ordinary. "Can you tell me why you're here with me now?"

Something touched my hair…something that might have been just a draft from the vent overhead, but which I guessed probably wasn't. The air seemed to grow even colder, and I watched as goosebumps prickled their way along my bare arms.

Then a single word.

"Gone."

And just like that, the spirit was gone as well. The sensation of ice that had seemed to encase me disappeared, and at the same time, the feeling of pressure on my chest and on my eardrums evaporated as well.

Enough fact finding for the day, I told myself, and fled down the stairs.

4

Musical Chairs

A FEW HOURS IN THE MUCH MORE MUNDANE surroundings of my shop helped to calm my nerves a bit, although I couldn't quite forget the spirit's whisper.

Gone.

What did that mean? True, the ghost was gone, or at least its corporeal body was no longer with us, but I had to believe it was trying to communicate something much more significant than that, something that tied into why it was still hanging around on this plane.

Unfortunately, without a bit more information than that single word, I doubted I'd be able to piece the story together.

I was definitely glad that I'd planned to close the store early, though, if for no other reason than it would feel good to be in my apartment with

Victoria Parrish as company. We would discuss normal, everyday things like caterers and linens and floral arrangements, and that should help to keep me settled until I could see Calvin later that evening and tell him exactly what had happened to me at the Bigelow mansion.

At least I didn't have to worry about him not believing me. After my adventures with Danny Ortega's ghost, Calvin was all too aware that my interactions with the spirit world were real, even if they weren't always precisely welcome.

Although I actually made a few sales that afternoon, I was still very relieved to put up the "be back at" sign in the front window a little after three-thirty, lock the door, and turn out the lights, then head upstairs to the apartment. Since I'd noticed the day before that Victoria liked iced tea, I made a pitcher and set it out with some short-bread cookies I'd baked a few days earlier. Nothing fancy, but I wanted to make sure she knew she was welcome in my home.

Archie watched these activities with a jaundiced eye. He really disliked visitors of any sort, even regulars like Hazel. But telling Victoria she couldn't come over would have been the height of rudeness, and so I reminded myself that my cursed cat needed to suck it up and not be so prickly.

I'd just set the pitcher of tea and plate of

cookies on the coffee table when a knock came at the door. Archie had been napping over by the window, and so he was somewhat trapped, since he would have had to bolt across the room to avoid my visitor and therefore make himself even more conspicuous.

"Hi, Victoria," I said, stepping aside to let her in.

"Hi, Selena," she replied, and followed me into the living room.

Almost at once, her gaze fell on Archie, still lying there in a pool of sunlight.

"Oh, what a gorgeous cat!" she exclaimed. "Can I pet him?"

Giving her permission would be an extraordinarily bad idea. Archie never allowed anyone to touch him—a painful lesson Hazel had learned after she got a couple of scratches when trying to stroke his ears.

"I'm sorry—Archie isn't very friendly," I said. "Probably better not to."

"Oh," Victoria replied, her expression falling. "That's too bad. I love cats—I lost my own kitty about a year ago, and I've been wanting to get another one. Just too busy right now, though."

I made a sound of commiseration as I sat down on the sofa. She started to follow me— and was brought up short, since Archie had gotten up from his sleeping position and was now winding himself around her legs, purring loudly.

What in the world?

Archie was never that friendly.

Never.

"I think he likes me," she said, and reached down to run a hand over his soft smoke-gray fur. His purrs increased, and I thought I saw his eyes slit in pleasure.

"Um...I guess so," I managed. Exactly what had brought about this utter change in behavior, I had no idea. The last time I'd seen him this out of whack was when I'd given him some catnip as a Christmas present, but I'd made sure never to have the feline narcotic in my house again after that episode. Archie was enough to handle sober; I definitely didn't need a continually stoned kitty.

Victoria gave him a final pat, then came over and sat down next to me on the couch. Archie followed, clearly ready to jump right into her lap.

"Archie, Victoria and I need to talk now," I said sternly. Since almost everyone I knew talked to their pets, I wasn't too worried about Victoria wondering why I was speaking to my cat as though he was an equal.

"Fine," he replied, and stalked off toward the office.

That one word had probably sounded like a hiss to Victoria, since, according to Archie, no one could understand his speech except witches, like me. Still, she smiled slightly.

"He sounds a little cranky."

"He's always cranky," I replied. "Iced tea?"

She accepted a glass, then declined my offer of sugar. "I drink it straight," she said with a hint of laughter in her bright blue eyes.

"Same here," I said, thinking more and more that we were going to get along just fine.

Well, except for the strange effect she seemed to have on my cursed cat.

After we each helped ourselves to a cookie, Victoria became all business. She reached for the binder I'd set out on the coffee table, the one filled with copies of Josie's and my notes, invoices, calendars, lists, and all the other minutiae of putting together an event that involved hundreds of guests. I'd known I'd have to surrender my personal folder, because you would have had to pry Josie's out of her cold, dead hands.

Which was fine. The whole point of this entire exercise was handing off everything to Victoria so I could relax and enjoy the process.

Of course, that would have been a lot easier if I hadn't just encountered an unexpected spirit hanging around the Bigelow mansion.

"Thanks so much," Victoria said as she flipped through the pages. "Josie said you're trying to work with local vendors as much as possible?"

"Yes," I replied. "The flowers are being done by a florist just down the street, and we're having the event catered by the restaurant at the Gold Dust casino."

And what a stroke of genius Calvin's suggestion had been. Not only did the casino's restaurant produce some pretty world-class food, but they were used to serving large numbers of people. At first I'd thought it might be fun to have the reception catered by Olamendi's, our favorite Mexican restaurant in town...except I realized fairly quickly that not only did they not have the capacity to create a sit-down dinner for two hundred people, the food itself was probably a little too casual for the sort of reception I'd envisioned.

I added, "Oh, and both the harpist for the ceremony and the band for the reception are local, so they won't be traveling very far, either."

"Perfect," Victoria said, quickly making a few notes on a blank page toward the back of the notebook. "That should make the logistics a little easier."

I nodded. "But the pavilions and all the seating and table linens, *et cetera* are coming from vendors in the Phoenix area. We just don't have anything like that here in Globe."

She nodded as she leafed through a few pages. "I understand. Well, I've worked with all these vendors before and they're very reliable, so I don't think you'll have anything to worry about."

Something Josie had already told me, but hearing it from Victoria made me feel a bit better. I'd sort of hated the idea of having to send so much of the business involved with the ceremony and the reception out of town, but tiny little Globe just couldn't support those sorts of specialized services. My plan had been to do as much as possible with vendors in my beloved adopted hometown, although reality had intervened more often than I would have liked.

Almost on cue, my cell phone rang. This close to the wedding, I didn't dare ignore a call, even when I had a guest, and so I murmured an apology to Victoria and hurried over to where I'd left my bag sitting on the dining room table.

The number was one I didn't recognize, with a Phoenix area code.

I put the phone to my ear. "Hello?"

"Selena Marx?"

A male voice, no one I'd ever heard before.

"Hey," he said. "I'm with Panorama Party Rentals. We're at the house to drop off your tables and chairs, but no one's here."

What the absolute hell? I blinked and said, "I'm afraid there must have been some sort of a mix-up. The chairs and tables weren't supposed to be delivered until next Thursday, June second."

A long pause. A scratchy, ruffling sound came through the speaker, probably the guy leafing through his work orders.

"Nope," he said. "It says right here, May twenty-sixth."

My heart fell. I didn't know who'd screwed up, but apparently now I had a truck loaded with chairs and tables for two hundred guests idling out at the Bigelow mansion, waiting to be off-loaded.

I'd been so wrapped up in the conversation, I hadn't even noticed that Victoria had approached. She nodded toward my phone and mouthed, *May I?*

Relieved to have an expert right there to handle the disaster, I handed over the phone. She lifted it to her ear.

"Hi," she said crisply. "This is Victoria Parrish, Selena's wedding planner. To whom am I speaking?" A pause, and then she went on, "I'm sorry, Dave, but this situation is not acceptable. The seating wasn't supposed to be delivered until next week. You'll just have to take it back to the warehouse and then come back next Thursday to set it up at the correct time."

She sounded brisk and efficient...and like the sort of person who wasn't about to take crap from anyone, belying her porcelain-doll appearance.

Then her brows drew together. Clearly, she

wasn't too happy with whatever this "Dave" was telling her.

"Hold on a minute," she said, and pulled the phone away so she could mute the microphone. "He says there'll be a five-hundred-dollar fee to take everything back to the warehouse."

I didn't really like the sound of that, but on the other hand, I could afford to take the hit.

"That's okay," I said in an undertone, even though I knew Dave couldn't hear what Victoria and I were saying.

Her mouth compressed. It seemed pretty clear to me she wasn't too happy about having a client shell out extra money for something that wasn't even her fault.

Then again…was it? Josie had been in charge of hiring the vendors for the pavilions and all the seating, so I supposed it was remotely possible she'd given the wrong date…although I really couldn't see my friend making that kind of obvious error. She was meticulous about that sort of thing.

Not that it mattered who was to blame. No, we just had to get this sorted out, one way or another.

Victoria unmuted the phone. "If that's what it takes—"

She stopped there; it seemed as though Dave had interjected something that didn't please her at all, because she frowned, her finely arched brows drawing together.

"There has to be some solution—" she began, and appeared to be cut off again. Frown deepening, she put the phone on mute again and said, "He just told me that isn't going to work. They actually ordered extra chairs because they thought you were going to be keeping them for so much longer than usual, and they can't take the stuff back to the warehouse because there isn't room… and also because all their trucks are going to be busy next Thursday delivering items for other events. It sounds as though half of Phoenix decided to get married on June fourth."

Not for the first time, I wanted to curse my lack of foresight in choosing that day for Calvin's and my wedding. It did seem to have some sort of badly aligned astrological aspects, even though I'd dutifully run the date through my astrology software to ensure we weren't going to have Uranus squaring Saturn or some equally unfortunate alignments on our big day.

Victoria went on, "He wants to know if there's someplace on the property where you can store everything. Then they should be able to send someone out next week to help set it up."

Right, because the Bigelow mansion had a warehouse tucked away on its back forty.

But then I remembered that, while it didn't

have a warehouse, it did have a large four-bay garage that was currently sitting empty. If we stored all the tables and chairs in there, Tom might not be able to park his Porsche SUV inside until after everything was set up for the reception, but still, that sounded better than having a bunch of the vendor's property sitting outside in the brutal sun.

"We can put everything in the garage," I said, then added quickly, "but it's locked. They'll have to wait until we can get out there and open it up."

Victoria relayed this information, and paused. The frown returned.

Apparently, Dave wasn't going to make this easy.

"They have another delivery to make and can't wait," she said. "They want to just leave everything in front of the garage, and then we can put the stuff away when we get there."

It appeared that Dave was angling for a one-star review on Yelp. But since it also seemed pretty clear there wasn't much I could do about the situation, I said, "Sure. Whatever. I can get Calvin and his brothers to help put it away once they're off work later this afternoon."

Not the best solution in the world, but I supposed that was one good thing about having a large family. There were always plenty of hands to pitch in when life decided to throw you a curveball.

"Okay, go ahead and do that," Victoria told Dave. "But I expect a little to be taken off the bill for the inconvenience."

She ended the call there and handed the phone back to me.

"What a mess," she said. "We should probably head over to the house to make sure they've at least left the correct number of tables and chairs."

"And if they haven't?" I asked.

"Then we'll call around to get replacements if necessary," she replied without missing a beat. "This is just a little hiccup. I wanted to go over to the house and walk the property with you anyway to get a feel for things, so this isn't that much of an inconvenience. Everything is going to be fine."

Considering what I'd experienced at that house just a couple of hours before, I sincerely hoped she was right.

We left right away, getting in Victoria's shiny red Mercedes SUV. I gave directions, and soon enough, we'd pulled up into the mansion's long gravel driveway.

And there were all the tables and chairs sitting in front of the big detached garage, only....

Victoria blinked as she shut off the engine. "Is this a joke?"

Yes, there were stacks of chairs, except they hadn't been stacked in the usual groups of four or six or even eight, but had been set one on top of the other in sets of what looked like twenty, reaching precariously high into the air. There was no way in the world either one of us could reach that high to start dismantling them. In fact, even Calvin and his brothers wouldn't be able to accomplish the task without bringing along a couple of ladders.

As I stared at those unnatural stacks of chairs, that familiar cold feeling returned to my spine.

Dave and the guys from the party supply company hadn't done this.

No, the ghost had.

I didn't know what was showing on my face right then, but my expression must have shifted, because Victoria asked, "Are you okay, Selena?"

"Not really," I managed, then hesitated. Part of me wanted to blurt out the truth, while the other was telling me I should keep my mouth shut and just pass this whole thing off as some kind of annoying joke.

Well, I'd never been very good at lying.

"There's something you need to know about the house," I said before I could lose my courage, and Victoria's eyebrows lifted behind the chic oversized sunglasses she wore.

"What's that?"

"I think it's haunted," I blurted out.

To my surprise, she didn't look too dismayed by this revelation. "Oh, really?" she replied. "Do you know the story behind the ghost? I just love hearing things about old houses like this."

Not exactly the response I'd been expecting, but I had to believe her reaction was an encouraging sign. At least she wasn't the kind of person to turn tail and run at the first sign of paranormal activity.

"No, I don't really know anything," I said. "I just know there's a presence here. And I'm pretty sure it was responsible for that."

I pointed at the insanely high stacks of chairs sitting in front of the garage.

To my surprise, Victoria's mouth curved into an amused smile. "Of course," she said. "No human being would stack chairs like that."

Her tone seemed to indicate she didn't believe me. I couldn't even be upset with her; most people wanted to look for the mundane explanation even when the paranormal one made the most sense.

"Would you?" I challenged her, and she shrugged.

"Probably not. But maybe they were stacked like that inside the truck to save space, and they had some sort of apparatus to lift them out in that same configuration."

On the surface, such an explanation sounded halfway plausible. Still....

"Have you ever seen Panorama Party Rentals use anything like that?" I asked. "I mean, you've worked with the company before, right?"

"I have," she said, still almost preternaturally calm. "But that doesn't mean they might not have upgraded their trucks or their equipment in the interim. Anyway, the important thing is that the tables and chairs are here, and they're definitely the ones you ordered. Let's just count them all to make sure they got that part right."

Since I didn't feel like arguing, I just nodded and went over and started counting tables, while she went from unnatural stack to unnatural stack to tally up all the chairs. At the end, we had exactly what had been ordered—twenty-five tables and two hundred and ten chairs.

"Well, that's handled at least," Victoria said. "Can we take a look inside the house?"

The last thing I wanted was to go in there. After all, if we were dealing with a spirit who could stack chairs like that, what would they do when I returned with a visitor? They definitely hadn't been very friendly the last time I was here, and with Josie down for the count, I'd really be up a creek if anything happened to my newly acquired wedding planner.

But I got the feeling Victoria wasn't in the mood for any more ghost stories, so I just shrugged. While the house wasn't officially being used for any part of the festivities, the plan was to keep it open so people could come inside and avail themselves of the restrooms on the ground floor. We'd also ordered some deluxe port-a-potties—more like fancy trailers—to be placed discreetly in a secluded spot on the grounds, but I had a feeling most people would rather wait in line inside than have to use one of those.

Well, at least the ghostly presence was much milder on the first floor of the house, so I had to hope our little inspection wouldn't be interrupted by some sort of weird phenomena.

Or maybe not. Maybe Victoria would be more likely to believe a ghost was inhabiting the house and capable of exerting its influence even out in the yard if she saw evidence of such powers with her own eyes. Despite her somewhat ethereal appearance, she definitely seemed like a no-nonsense sort of person.

"Sure, let's take a look," I said, and started up the flagstone path that led to the front door, the wedding planner a pace or two behind me. Even though she wore another of her chic sheath dresses today, her sandals had much lower heels than the ones she'd had on for her meeting with me and Josie the day before, indicating that she'd known we might have to hike around a bit to explore the mansion's grounds.

As before, cool air drifted out as soon as I opened the front door. When I stepped inside, however, I didn't catch even a whiff of the ghostly presence I'd detected yesterday. Frowning, I moved closer to the stairwell and laid a hand on the carved newel post.

Nope, nothing.

"What an absolutely gorgeous home!" Victoria exclaimed. "It's really rare that you find something this well-preserved, especially here in Arizona." She walked into the front parlor and ran an admiring hand over the heavy mahogany mantel-piece, then turned around toward me, her expression becoming businesslike. "Do you have any plans for flowers in here?"

"Um…no," I said. Honestly, I'd thought it enough simply to allow people to come inside, and hadn't really thought about sprucing up the interior of the mansion to coordinate with the wedding theme.

Her brow furrowed slightly, but then she sent me an encouraging smile. "Well, that's all right. I'll call the florist and see if we can get some arrangements for the mantel here, and also for that side table at the foot of the stairs. Nothing too much, but enough to show we're welcoming people in here."

I had to hope that Florence Mills, the florist at Everything's Coming Up Roses who was doing all the floral arrangements, would be able to squeeze in a few more bouquets. Yes, she had an assistant, but still, the order for the Standingbear-Marx wedding was probably one of the biggest her shop had ever handled.

"Okay," I replied. Victoria was the expert and I wasn't, so I intended to go along with most of her suggestions…although I'd draw the line at any advice to release a hundred doves the second Calvin and I shared our first kiss as a married couple. "Was there anything else you needed to see?"

"Just want to check out the kitchen," she responded as she began to move down the hallway toward the back of the house.

"The caterers are setting up an outdoor kitchen," I said, my tone dubious.

"True, but it's always good to know what we're working with in case there's an emergency."

Since I couldn't really come up with a rebuttal to that completely sensible statement, I followed her into the kitchen. Once again, her gaze was approving as she looked over the professional-grade stainless-steel appliances and the slightly glittery quartz countertops.

"Very nice," she said. "Not that we could prepare food for a sit-down meal for two hundred people in here, but it's certainly enough that it would work as a pinch-hitter as necessary." She stopped there, gaze moving upward, and I stiffened.

Had she heard something?

Apparently not, because in the next moment she smiled and said, "Well, I think that's it for the house. Let's do a quick circuit of the grounds, just so I can see the real-life version of what you and Josie laid out in your paperwork, and I think that should just about do it."

I was more than happy to get the heck out of the house, even though I hadn't sensed a single supernatural flutter since I'd crossed the threshold. Just because it was quiet now didn't mean it would stay that way.

So we went and walked through the gardens, with Victoria occasionally pausing to snap some photos with the camera on her iPhone. Out here, it was almost hard to believe that I'd experienced something so strange in the house just the day before…or that the chairs the party-supply people had delivered had been stacked in such an abnormal way.

But those stacks were still there when we walked back over to Victoria's car. Mimicking her, I took a couple of quick shots of the chairs, just so

Calvin and his brothers would know what they were getting into when I assigned them the task of moving everything into the garage.

I sent the text as we drove back into town, followed with, *I'm really sorry about this. I don't know why the chairs were stacked that way, but I hope you and your brothers can handle it.*

My response was a grin emoji and, *No worries. We'll bring a crane.*

The only real way to answer was with the tongue-sticking-out emoji. All the same, I had to be relieved. Calvin had accepted this crazy situation with the same equanimity he seemed to employ no matter what madness might be intruding on my life at the time, and I had to be grateful for that. Not for the first time, I reflected how lucky I'd been to stumble across a gem like him tucked away in this unassuming small town.

Victoria came up to the apartment with me, since she needed to retrieve the notebooks she'd left sitting on the coffee table. Just as she was done tucking them under one arm, Archie emerged from the office, where presumably he'd been getting his beauty sleep.

Once again, Victoria bent down to pet him, and once again he appeared to willingly submit to her caresses.

What the heck was going on?

But then she headed over to the door and we

said our goodbyes, with her assuring me she was going to follow up with all the other vendors to make sure we wouldn't have any more mishaps like the one that had just occurred with Panorama Party Supply.

"And I'm just five minutes away in my Airbnb," she added. "So feel free to call if you have any questions or even if you're starting to feel jittery. That's what I'm here for."

I wanted to tell her the only thing that was making me jittery was the possible presence of ghosts in the Bigelow mansion, but I decided that probably wasn't a very good idea. I certainly wasn't nervous about getting married to Calvin. When it came to making our commitment to each other permanent, that special day couldn't come soon enough.

"Thanks," I said. "I think it's all going to be fine."

"I'll ensure it will," Victoria replied. "Can we meet for lunch tomorrow? I'd like to go over a few more things."

"Absolutely."

We agreed to meet at Olamendi's at noon, and then she headed out. After I closed the door, I turned back to look at Archie, who'd remained sitting on the living room rug.

"Do you want to tell me what all that was about?" I inquired.

He was staring at the shut door with what I could only describe as a moony expression on his feline features. Then he stirred and looked up at me.

"Who was that divine creature?"

5

Crushing It

"'DIVINE CREATURE'?" I ECHOED, STARING AT him in mystification. "You mean Victoria?"

"Yes."

I blinked. "Her name is Victoria Parrish. She's the wedding planner Josie hired to come in and help me, since she won't be very mobile with a broken ankle."

Another blink of Archie's big golden eyes. "'Victoria,'" he repeated in musing tones. "A perfect name for a perfect creature."

My cursed cat must have hidden a stash of catnip somewhere in the house. That was the only reasonable explanation for his current behavior. Never in all the months I'd known him had I seen Archie evince even the slightest bit of interest in a member of the opposite sex—or his own sex, either. He'd told me he'd been asexual when he was a man, but now I was starting to wonder if he hadn't been entirely truthful with me.

"You think she's pretty?" I asked innocently, figuring I might as well play along and see how much he tripped himself up.

"'Pretty'?" he said in tones dripping with scorn. "She's an utter goddess."

I had to admit that Victoria Parrish was beautiful, with the sort of porcelain-perfect looks that would have made her a shoo-in to play some sort of Regency-era heroine, all slender empire-style gowns and artfully curled locks escaping just so from a period up-do. Had the brides she'd worked with been jealous of her beauty? I'd noticed she was very put together, but in a simple, no-fuss sort of way, with minimal makeup and jewelry and only clear polish on her manicured nails.

All qualities that might be the perfect combination to attract the interest of someone as conservative and set in his ways as Archie.

Well, except for that little bit about him claiming to be asexual.

"I thought you weren't into women," I said, deciding to just put it on the table and see where we went from there.

"I'm not," the cat replied at once, then paused, an expression of utter confusion passing over his face. "Or at least, I didn't think I was." His tail flicked back and forth, a sure sign of agitation.

Then he uttered four words I'd never thought I'd hear leave his lips. "I just don't know."

Since he seemed so obviously upset, I didn't think it would be a good idea to push him further. "Well, Victoria is a very nice person, so I'd say you have good taste."

"'Good taste'?" he repeated, ears swiveling. "I shouldn't have 'taste' at all."

And before I could respond, he stalked off toward the laundry room.

Better to let him go. Clearly, he had his own stuff to work out…but that didn't mean I couldn't try to do my best to figure this out on my own.

Luckily, Hazel dropped in midway through the afternoon. I'd texted her to let her know about Victoria, and her relieved response told me all I needed to know about what might have happened if the two of us had attempted to manage the wedding on our own.

But once I was done telling my friend about Victoria and the few minor tweaks she had planned for the ceremony and reception, I ventured, "Hazel, have you ever heard of someone being asexual and then turning around and realizing they're attracted to someone?"

Her hazel eyes—I didn't know if her parents

had given her that name because of them, but they suited her perfectly—glinted a little. She wore her usual uniform of a paint-spattered T-shirt and loose faded jeans, but still managed to look like the quintessential gorgeous girl next door.

"Is there something you haven't been telling me, Selena?"

I grinned. "Nope, totally heterosexual female over here. This is more of a…hypothetical. Something I've been researching."

For a second, I wondered if she was going to ask me exactly why I'd been conducting that sort of research, but apparently she decided to put her questions aside. "Well, you know how sexuality is a spectrum, right? And there are people along that spectrum who are demisexual, graysexual…people who really aren't into it until they meet the one person who rings their bell, so to speak. It's really not that unusual."

My expression must have been questioning, because she gave a lift of her shoulders before continuing.

"I knew someone like that in college. He absolutely had no interest in anyone…until he met this one guy, and the rest was history. I guess they're married now and are in the middle of restoring this big old house they bought on the outskirts of Des Moines."

So, Archie's reaction to Victoria Parrish wasn't as uncommon as I might have thought. And since I was a firm believer in the universe sending us the things we needed precisely when we needed them, then I had to think that maybe he'd had to spend so many years in a cat's body because it would take that long for exactly the one right person to finally cross his path.

Which meant that Josie's broken ankle was also fate, an aspect of the situation I didn't find quite as appealing. I didn't like the idea of someone I cared about getting hurt just so Archie could meet his one true love.

But here we all were, so I'd just have to roll with it…and also roll with the sad fact that Archie was still living in a cat's body, and there didn't seem to be much I could do to change the situation.

"You're sure this is just for research?" Hazel probed, and I nodded, probably too vigorously.

"Yes. I was reading about someone's situation on a witchy Facebook page I follow, and I was a little confused, since I'd never come across circumstances like that before."

To my relief, this explanation seemed to suffice, because my friend let it go. We chatted a bit, and I invited her along to my lunch with Victoria at Olamendi's the next day, figuring it would be a good idea for the wedding planner and the maid-of-honor to meet. With that matter settled, Hazel headed out.

A little while after that, I got a text from Calvin letting me know he and his brothers had managed to take down all the weird stacks of chairs and secure everything in the garage. He had his own set of keys to the house, since my mother and Tom had thought it would be a good idea in case he ever needed to head over there without me, and so it hadn't been necessary for him to waste time driving all the way to the store to get them from me.

I thanked him but left the matter there. We were getting together for dinner later in the day anyway, and I figured it was better to leave any discussions about possible ghosts aside until we could talk in person.

After I locked up the store and went upstairs to the apartment, I found Archie sitting in front of the living room window, staring moodily down at Broad Street below.

"Hey," I said. "Salmon feast for dinner tonight?"

He slowly turned around and sent me a scathing glance. "Oh, yes, that will make everything better."

Clearly, he was in one of his funks. Not that I could blame him, since I had a pretty good idea as to the source of his current sour mood.

"I'm still a cat," he pointed out, and I nodded.

"Yes," I said. "Sorry about that."

His nose wrinkled. "'Sorry'? That's the best you can do?"

I set down my purse and moved into the living room. He remained where he was, golden eyes glowing with annoyance.

"Unfortunately, it's the only thing I can do," I said quietly. "I'm still chasing down some books that might help, and I'll keep trying until I've exhausted every possible resource, but I'm not a miracle worker."

"No," he retorted. "You're a very sorry witch."

And he stalked past me, tail high, obviously headed for the office.

With some effort, I remained silent. This wasn't the first time Archie had cast aspersions on my talents as a witch, and I doubted it would be the last. Problem was, I could tell him until I was blue in the face that I simply wasn't that kind of witch, that my talents lay in divination and mani-festation, not turning people into cats...or turning cats back into men. In the end, he wanted me to be something I wasn't, and I knew I couldn't do much to manage his expectations except keep trying in my own way to do what I could to help him.

Since I had a little time before I needed to be over at Calvin's place, I probably could have gotten out my Tarot deck or my pendulum to see if the universe was ready to offer me some guidance on the problem of Archie Bradshaw and Victoria Parrish. Unfortunately, reaching out to the universe to see what sort of answers it might provide wasn't going to happen right then, not with Archie holed up in the office where I kept my altar and all my divination tools.

Instead, I opened a can of salmon feast and put it in Archie's bowl, and quietly let myself out.

I had time to kill…and I knew exactly where I needed to kill it.

Pulling up to the garage at the mansion and seeing all the tables and chairs put away did help to improve my mood a little. My heart still hurt for Archie, and yet I also knew that beating myself up wasn't going to magically improve the situation. He would need to work through this very unexpected wrinkle on his own, although of course I would try to lend him as much emotional support as possible.

The gardens lay serene under a bright blue sky, now looking slightly gilded as the sun began to slip down toward the horizon. There was absolutely nothing here to indicate anything was wrong with the big house that stood in the center of all this gorgeousness, and yet I knew better than most how much could lie unseen beneath the surface.

But I'd been here earlier in the day, and nothing had happened. Maybe it was Victoria's presence and nothing more; ghosts could be notoriously unpredictable and sensitive to people's vibrations, and it seemed entirely possible that she was just too down-to-earth and sensible for a spirit to want to manifest in her presence. Whatever the reason for the ghost's silence during our lunchtime foray to the mansion, I wanted to see whether it would remain resolutely quiet…or whether it might have a little more to say if I came back here alone.

I had about fifteen minutes before I needed to get in my car and head down the hill to Calvin's house. The strict timeframe reassured me more than anything else, since it meant I wouldn't feel compelled to linger here, trying to get some sort of response from the ghost.

If there was even one at all. My imagination could have been playing tricks on me, trying to manufacture something that simply wasn't there.

No, that hypothesis didn't feel right. Something was definitely in this house. Later on, I could puzzle out why it had chosen this particular moment in time to manifest, but for now, I just wanted a second data point.

I'd only been here a few hours earlier, but as soon as I walked into the mansion, I could tell something was different. Right inside the door was an eddy of cold air that hadn't been there during Victoria's and my visit, and once again, it felt as though something played with the ends of my hair before moving on.

"Who are you?" I asked. "What are you doing in this place?"

No reply...not that I'd really been expecting one. However, a strange tingle at the back of my neck seemed to propel me toward the front parlor, where I saw one of the heavy velvet drapes at the window move just the tiniest fraction, as though someone had pushed it out of the way to get a better view of the front walk outside.

Almost the movement of someone waiting to see a visitor come up the walkway I'd traversed just a few minutes earlier, although who or what the spirit was waiting for, I couldn't begin to guess.

Just as I had the day before, I said, "I'd like to help you."

The curtain moved again. I couldn't see anything there, but I got the feeling that the ghost had turned toward me, releasing the velvet drape it had held a moment earlier.

A whisper of a sigh.

No.

Well, that wasn't very encouraging. Then again, I wasn't a medium. I wasn't someone who specialized in speaking to the souls of the departed, even if I had a little experience in that area.

But Lucien Dumond's ghost had been almost incoherent, his speech nearly drowned out by his rage at being murdered by his brother and betrayed by the woman he'd thought cared for him, and Danny Ortega's spirit had been so relentlessly normal that hanging out with him hadn't felt very different from being with him when he was alive.

This situation seemed entirely dissimilar.

I glanced down at my watch. About seven or eight minutes before I had to leave.

A small breath to give me courage, and then I said, "Do you mean no, you don't want my help, or no, I can't help you?"

Stubborn silence was my only answer.

Great.

This did seem like the perfect situation to call in a medium and see if they would be able to offer any sort of concrete help, since I certainly didn't seem to be getting anywhere. On the other hand, I could just imagine my mother's reaction if I told her I'd discovered the house was haunted and we needed expert assistance…especially because I'd assured her months earlier that the house didn't have any sort of ghostly presences and was perfectly safe to live in.

Which it had been, up until just this week. All those Airbnbers, all the workmen coming in and out to perform repairs after the demon-infestation scheme had been found out the summer before… no one had seen a darn thing.

Just for the barest flicker of a second, so quickly my eyes barely managed to register it was there at all, I caught the faintest hint of a woman standing by the window. A girl, really, probably ten years younger than I or even more. She wore a lacy white dress, slim in cut, which I thought looked as though it might have been from the late teens or early 1920s, if my memory of the costumes from *Downton Abbey* was at all accurate, and she was pretty in a delicate sort of way, with big pale eyes and flaxen hair pulled into a low knot at the back of her neck.

And just as quickly, she was gone.

My breath caught, and I hurried into the parlor, then reached out and touched the curtain. No trace of cold here, the velvet soft and warm beneath my fingertips, but I still shuddered.

She'd been here. I'd seen her.

Now I just had to figure out who the heck she was…and what she wanted.

"Haunted?" Calvin said.

Once again, we sat in his backyard, the wonderful aroma of chicken shish-kebabs grilling in the background, the warm late afternoon sun falling on our faces. It all felt safe and normal and very far away from the Victorian mansion that appeared to have one more resident than I'd thought.

"'Haunted,'" I repeated. "I saw her. Just for a split-second, but she was there. And I heard her voice as well, just like I did the day before yesterday. Not that she's very talkative…last time it was 'gone,' and this time it was 'no.'"

"Any idea who she is?" Calvin asked. To my relief, he hadn't tried to poke holes in my story, or tell me I was seeing things that weren't there. If I said a house was haunted, well, then it was.

I lifted my glass of pinot grigio and took a sip. It flowed over my tongue, tart and cool and exactly what I needed right then. "None at all," I replied. "She doesn't sound like anyone Josie described to me as being part of the Bigelow family, and yet she must have been. Her clothes looked like they were from sometime in the 1920s or maybe even the late teens, which means the Bigelows would have still owned the place at that point."

Calvin sipped some of his own wine, then got up from his chair at the patio table to go over and rotate the shish-kebabs a precise inch. That man took his barbecuing seriously.

"Is it possible she was a family friend or a neighbor who died there?"

I considered his question for a moment, then gave a helpless lift of my shoulders. "Maybe? Usually ghosts don't haunt a place unless they have a strong emotional attachment to the location, and that's why they tend to hang around places where they lived. I suppose if this girl died violently in the house, then that would be a reason for her to be haunting it. But Josie never mentioned anything about something like that happening in the Bigelow mansion."

This response got me a lift of the eyebrow, as if Calvin wanted to question my faith in Josie Woodrow's knowledge of local history. He apparently decided that wasn't a very good idea, however, probably because he knew as well as I did that what Josie didn't know about Globe could fit in a thimble. If a young woman had lost her life in some kind of accident or actual crime on the property, she would have told me about it.

"Maybe no one knew about her," he suggested.

"How would that even be possible?" I returned. All right, I had to admit it had probably been a lot easier to cover up scandals and even crimes back in the days before the internet and social media, but still, I had to think that in a small, tight-knit community like Globe, it would be a fairly difficult task.

His shoulders lifted, and he turned the shish-kebabs once again—not because they necessarily needed it, but because Calvin was the sort of person who needed to move around and do things while he was cogitating.

After a long pause, he said, "I honestly don't know. But if the house is really haunted—"

"It is," I cut in, my voice firm. "I know what I saw and heard. I still don't know why the ghost has appeared now when she seems to have been dormant in the past."

"I thought Hank and Nora told everyone the house was haunted," Calvin replied, referring to the previous owners of the Bigelow mansion, people who'd resided there for more than forty years before deciding the place was too much for them and selling it so they could retire to a condo in Scottsdale.

"They did," I said, and sipped some of my pinot grigio. "But it turned out they'd invented those stories to make the house seem more appealing. I mean, what kind of self-respecting historic home doesn't have its own resident ghost?"

Calvin smiled, but I could tell the wheels were still turning in his brain. "What if they weren't making them up?"

I hadn't even thought about that. To be fair, I hadn't heard any of the information about the Bigelow mansion's *faux* ghost directly, but had only gotten the stories secondhand from Josie and from Al Loomis. And since Al was now in prison, convicted of second-degree murder in the death of Brant Thoreau, I couldn't exactly count him as a reliable witness. For all I knew, he'd glossed over the accounts from Hank and Nora Anders because in the back of his mind, he'd still been hoping that I might harbor a suspicion that the demons he and Miriam had cooked up together might have had some basis in reality.

Clearly, I needed to go to the source. I didn't have Hank and Nora's contact information, but I knew who would.

Josie Woodrow.

"I know that glint in your eye," Calvin said then. "What are you cooking up now?"

No point in trying to pretend I hadn't already been making plans—my fiancé knew me far too well for that.

"I'm thinking that I need to talk to Josie so I can get the Anders' phone number from her," I replied calmly. "Then I can talk to them and ask if they'd ever seen the same woman I saw in the front parlor this afternoon."

Judging by the way the Calvin's brows pulled

together right then, I got the feeling he wasn't too thrilled with this scheme.

"You do remember that we're getting married a week from tomorrow, right?" he asked.

"Yes," I said. "But I also have Victoria to do all the heavy lifting, so I don't see how this is going to interfere too much. Besides, I'm only planning on making a quick phone call. Anyway, since I'm the daughter of the mansion's new owners, it shouldn't seem that weird for me to be following up on any information about its ghosts."

Silence for a moment as Calvin seemed to weigh that argument. It appeared I'd won him over, because he finally shrugged and said, "If you really think it's going to help."

As to that, I couldn't say for sure. All I knew was that I needed to start somewhere...and the Anders seemed to be the most logical place to begin.

6

Gossip Girls

JOSIE SEEMED A LITTLE SURPRISED BY MY inquiry about Hank and Nora's contact info. I'd called her Friday morning, wishing I had the time to go visit her in person, but knowing my lunch hour was already promised to Hazel and Victoria.

"You really think the mansion is haunted?" Josie asked. From the excitement in her voice, it sounded as though she thought that was a good thing. Maybe ghosts boosted real estate values… not that my mother and Tom were planning to sell the Bigelow mansion any time in the near future.

"I'm pretty sure," I replied. "But I've gotten so much conflicting information about whether or not it had ghosts that it seems the smartest thing to do is to talk to the people who lived there for forty years."

A pause. Then Josie said, "I wish I could give you Nora's number, but that's handing out client information, and I don't want to upset her. Is it all right if I give her a call and let her know what's going on, and then have her call you?"

It wasn't the best of solutions, but it was better than nothing. "Sure," I said. "Just let her know this is kind of time-sensitive, since I'd really like to get this figured out before the wedding, if at all possible."

"Of course," Josie said immediately. "How is everything going with Victoria? She texted me to let me know she'd walked the property with you and thought it was amazing, but she didn't give me any real details."

Probably better not to mention how my cursed cat had developed an unlikely crush on the pretty wedding planner. "Oh, she's great," I replied. "Really on top of things, has great ideas. I feel like I'm in good hands."

I couldn't see Josie, of course, but I got the feeling she was beaming at this report. "That's great to hear. I knew she would be a good fit."

"She's wonderful," I said. "How's your ankle?"

A sigh came through the speaker. "About as well as possible, I suppose. Brett took me to my doctor's appointment this morning, and the doctor said I'm healing up just fine but need to stay off it as much as possible. That's not the easiest thing to manage, of course, living alone like I do, but Brett and Terry have been a big help. It does look as though I'll be on crutches by the time your wedding gets here, though, so at least I won't have to worry about having Brett roll me all over the place."

That did sound like good news. Obviously, Josie wouldn't be able to roam all the places on the grounds where we planned to have little seating areas and nooks set up, but the grassy lawn where the ceremony itself would be held was fairly flat, and so was the spot about twenty yards away where the main party pavilion would be erected. She should be able to get around pretty well on crutches as long as she didn't get too ambitious.

"I'm so glad," I told her. A woman who looked as though she was in her middle forties, wearing cargo pants and an Arizona Cardinals T-shirt, entered the store, and so I added quickly, "I need to go, but I'll let you know what I hear from Nora."

"Thanks for the call!" Josie chirped, and then hung up.

I set my phone down on the little shelf beneath the cash register, then went out to assist my one and only customer. She ended up buying several books and a set of agate bookends, so the interruption was definitely welcome.

And then it was time to close up and head

over to Olamendi's. I'd already put out Archie's food, and so he was taken care of...although I thought I detected a hint of jealousy in his eyes when I told him I was meeting Victoria Parrish for lunch. Obviously, there was no way he could come along on that particular outing, since while I'd seen people bring service dogs into restaurants, there didn't seem to be such a thing as a service cat.

Just as well. I wasn't sure I could trust him to behave himself around his newfound crush.

Hazel was already there, and had snagged our favorite table. I settled myself into a chair next to her, glad that I'd walked and so could treat myself to a margarita if I so desired. "How's it going?" she asked. "I figured the lack of frantic phone calls means things are working out with Victoria."

"Oh, she's great," I said, echoing what I'd just told Josie. "I'm pretty sure it's going to be smooth sailing...or at least, it would be if I didn't have a ghost interfering with the process."

"A what?" Hazel responded, her expression clearly startled.

Briefly, I explained the situation with the chairs, and how I'd seen the young woman in antique dress for just a split-second before she disappeared. "I'm waiting on a call from Nora Anders to see if she can shed any light on the situation," I concluded. "Because I've got enough on my plate without worrying about what this ghost —if that's really what she is—plans to do next."

Hazel made a sympathetic noise. Like Calvin, she'd been around me long enough to understand the paranormal seemed to trail in my wake like a cloud of too-heavy perfume. Before she could say anything, though, Victoria appeared, looking as pulled-together and chic as the other times I'd seen her. I had to admit her slim white slacks and pink sleeveless silk blouse made Hazel's V-neck T-shirt and jeans appear just a little too casual, although I'd be the first to admit that Olamendi's wasn't exactly a dress-up kind of place.

I made the introductions, and Victoria took the empty seat to Hazel's right. "I got the extra flowers squared away with the florist," she told us. "So that's handled. And I confirmed the deliveries of the pavilions and the extra seating, so I don't think we need to worry about any of that."

Hazel's brows lifted slightly at the mention of extra flowers, but apparently she didn't see any reason to pursue the subject. Like me, she was just glad to have an expert managing all the details… and I had no doubt she was taking some mental notes and thinking she might want to hire Victoria for her own big day. As far as I could tell, Hazel and Chuck wanted to have their wedding on his ranch, since there a ton of space and doing that rather than renting a different venue would save them a chunk of change, but even so, having someone to take care of the minutiae had to be pretty appealing.

"What do you think of the site?" she inquired instead, expression just slightly arch, as though she'd asked the question because she wanted to see whether Victoria would mention anything about the ghost.

"Oh, it's just lovely," Victoria said. "And really, the plans Josie and Selena came up with were perfect, so all I have to do is make sure that vision becomes a reality." She paused there, expression turning amused. "Assuming we don't have any more incidents like what happened with the chairs."

"Right," Hazel replied. "Selena told me about that. It sounds like the Bigelow mansion's ghost is acting up a little."

At once, Victoria's brows drew together. Corners of her mouth still slightly curved in amusement, she said, "Oh, I was just talking about the mix-up with the party-supply company. You don't honestly think there's a ghost, do you?"

Hazel was saved from making a reply by the arrival of Rosa, the restaurant's owner. She often handled waitress duties during the slower times, and she took our orders for margaritas—well, margaritas for Hazel and me, and a glass of iced tea for Victoria—then said she'd give us a few more minutes to look over the menu while she got the drinks together. This offer was clearly intended for our guest, since both Hazel and I practically had that menu memorized.

Once that was handled, though, Hazel settled back in her chair, her own mouth quirking just a bit.

"Oh, sure," she said easily. "All kinds of crazy stuff follows Selena around. Or did you not do that particular bit of research?"

I shot Hazel an evil glare, but she just continued to wear that half smile.

To be fair, she hadn't said anything that wasn't true.

"You mean the murders?" Victoria responded, obviously unruffled. "Yes, I saw all that when I Googled Selena's name. But there wasn't anything supernatural about any of those crimes…just horrible luck, I suppose."

On the surface, it probably did look that way. After all, there hadn't been anything paranormal about Lucien Dumond's death, or about Lilith Black's…or Dillon James' murder, which was definitely the crime that had gotten the most national attention. Those had all been simple cases of personal betrayal and nothing more.

But Athene Kappas, Lucien's assistant, had died when the car she was riding in had a solo rollover, thanks to a particularly nasty hex set on the vehicle. That wasn't the sort of thing a newspaper would report, though. To anyone who hadn't known what was really going on, it would have simply looked like a terrible accident.

And Danny's death really had been a horrible mistake and nothing else. Because it hadn't been a spectacular murder, his passing hadn't really been picked up by the Phoenix news media, and certainly no one knew I'd spent the greater part of a week being followed around by his ghost.

"There's still a lot more going on than meets the eye," I said calmly. "And because I think I saw the spirit who's hanging around the Bigelow mansion, I'm trying to find out what I can about her."

For the first time, Victoria appeared to falter a bit. She seemed to go pale under her light golden tan and said, "You saw it…I mean, her? When?"

I nodded, then paused as Rosa approached with our tray of drinks. After she'd set them down in front of us—and after we'd all placed our orders—I figured it was safe to continue.

"Yesterday afternoon," I replied, then paused to sip some of my peach margarita. Since I had to be back at work after this, I didn't dare have more than the one drink, but it sure tasted good. "She was in the front parlor and then disappeared. It looked like she was wearing a dress from the 1920s, something like that."

"A member of the Bigelow family?" Victoria asked.

I shook my head, then took another sip of my margarita. "I don't think so. From what I've been able to gather, Jack Bigelow, who built the house, had two sons. They probably would have been around the right age, but this was definitely a woman I saw, not a man. I'm planning to talk to one of the people who owned the place before my parents bought it to see if they have any information."

Victoria absorbed all this, and then finally reached for her glass of iced tea so she could help herself to some. "It sounds like an interesting story," she said. "I hope you can find something that will help you put the pieces together."

I hoped so, too. At the same time, I had to appreciate how she hadn't told me I shouldn't be wasting my energy on this sort of thing so close to the wedding...probably because she knew that with her on board to manage all the details, I honestly didn't have that much to do. The invitations had been sent months ago, and everything had been ordered and scheduled and planned. About the most I'd have to do was play hostess when Tom's family arrived, something I really wasn't looking forward to. More than once, I'd wondered how such a nice guy could have such obnoxious children. They must have taken after their mother, a woman Tom had divorced years before.

But at least they were staying at the mansion and so should be mostly out of my hair. No, probably the most I'd really have to deal with was pretending to be nice to them at the rehearsal dinner, which was being held at the Gold Dust casino's restaurant. I loved Olamendi's, but I could just imagine Madison's reaction to holding such an event at what was basically a hole-in-the-wall Mexican place.

"We'll just have to see," I went on. "But in the meantime, I think I'm going to go back and smudge the house, just to be safe."

"Will that work?" Hazel asked then. I wouldn't say she looked completely dubious, but still.

On the one hand, I could kind of understand her skepticism. I'd smudged and purified the heck out of the house the previous summer when I'd thought demons were residing there, and that didn't seem to have done much to keep the ghost away.

"It couldn't hurt," I replied. "I'd actually planned to do it anyway, just because it's always good to get the energies of a place sorted out before a lot of people invade the space. And also, smudging isn't a one-and-done kind of thing. There've been multiple guests coming and going after the past few months, and so it probably needs a good cleansing."

My friend accepted this explanation without comment—probably because she was all too used to my woo-woo practices by this point—while Victoria still looked sort of puzzled but didn't seem ready to interject her own opinion.

Probably from long practice in pretending the bride was always right, even if she secretly didn't believe a word of it.

Well, it didn't matter whether Victoria believed me or not. Smudging was a time-honored way to purify a space and make sure its energies were clear and not jangly. I did it in my apartment and the store once a month, just to be safe.

Then again, all the purification in the world didn't seem to have made Archie any less cranky.

The food arrived, and we all settled down to eating. As the meal progressed, we moved on to topics that were a little less fraught, like our girls' day out in Gilbert this coming Thursday, and exactly when Hazel needed to arrive at the mansion for the all-important primping session before the wedding. Because the house was so big, the bridal party would take over the smaller of the two ground-floor salons to get ready, and that was where the makeup artists and hairstylists would have their stations. At Josie's advice, I'd hired people from the greater Phoenix area, because, while the two hair salons in Globe were good for trims and basic color—and prom up-dos, I supposed—she didn't think they were quite at the level an event like Calvin's and my wedding deserved.

All the pieces had been set up. Now I just had to hope they'd be in the proper place when the big day arrived.

After lunch, I headed back to the shop, while Hazel went home to get back to work on her current painting and Victoria returned to her Airbnb. It sounded as though she'd set up her own office there, and was working in the background on the upcoming weddings she was managing in between all the tasks she had to handle for my own nuptials.

Which was fine. I certainly didn't expect her to dedicate every single hour of the day to the Standingbear-Marx ceremony.

A little after two, the phone rang—my cell phone, not the store's landline. I didn't recognize the number, which had a Phoenix area code, but that didn't stop me from answering. Even if it wasn't Nora Anders, I still had a ton of vendors who might be reaching out to get in contact for one reason or another.

When I answered, though, I heard an older woman's voice say, "Is this Selena Marx?"

"Yes, it's Selena," I said, and paused as a man and a woman around my own age walked past the store's picture window. However, they kept going, and I allowed myself to relax.

"Hi, Selena," the woman said. "This is Nora Anders."

"Oh, hi, Nora," I responded, hoping I didn't sound too eager. After all, I didn't want to scare her off before we even got started. "Thanks so much for calling me."

"It's nothing," Nora said. "That is, I figured I owed your family something, after all the mess they went through with the house."

"That wasn't your fault."

A small hesitation, and then she said, "Well, maybe not all of it, but Hank and I did recommend Al Loomis to do the home inspection. I can't help but think it might not have been so bad if he hadn't been involved from the start."

I hadn't really thought about the situation from that angle, but as far as I was concerned, it was all water under the bridge at this point. "It's okay," I assured her. "We got it all straightened out in the end, which is the important thing. But I was really hoping you could tell me more about the Bigelow ghost. I've gotten conflicting stories."

Nora paused again. When she spoke, however,

she didn't sound hesitant, but almost cheerful, as if talking about the ghost brought up happy memories from the decades she and her husband had lived in the house.

"Oh, she's definitely there," Nora said.

"'She'?" I asked at once, pouncing on that small tidbit. "You saw her?"

"No," Nora replied immediately, and I deflated just a little. I'd really been hoping the home's former owner could corroborate what I myself had seen.

"Then how did you know it was a woman?"

"I can't say for sure," Nora said. "That is, something about her presence just felt female, I suppose. She would move things around, but she never did anything malicious. It sometimes felt almost playful, like the time she left Hank's glasses in the fruit bowl on the dining room table, or how she kept blowing out the candles on the mantel when we were getting ready to have family over for Christmas. And once or twice, I could almost swear I smelled her perfume."

That was interesting. While ghosts sometimes had olfactory phenomena associated with them, it was a much rarer occurrence than cold spots or moving objects from place to place or even faint glimpses of movement in the shadows or from the corner of your eye. "What kind of perfume?" I asked.

"It smelled like lemon verbena to me," Nora replied. "Something soft and old-fashioned like that. I suppose it could have just been my imagination, or thinking the furniture polish smelled like perfume, but I don't think so. It would come as drifts in the downstairs front parlor sometimes, although the place I smelled it the most was the big bedroom upstairs, the one we were using as an office."

A small shiver worked its way down my spine.

The office was the exact same place where I'd caught my own glimpse of the ghost. Had that been her bedroom, once upon a time? It was certainly the nicest one on that floor—other than the master suite, of course—and would have been suitable for the only daughter of the house.

Well, except for the troublesome little fact that Jack Bigelow and his wife had had only sons, and not a daughter.

"Do you have any idea who she might have been?" I asked, even though I knew trying to get that information out of Nora was a long shot. "A family friend? A relative?"

I could almost see Nora's shrug. "I really have no idea. Hank and I talked about it a lot—we were fascinated by the family that had lived there before us, and so we did as much research as we were able. She definitely doesn't sound as though she looks like Jack Bigelow's daughter-in-law, the one who married his son Sam. Anyway, the two of them were happily married for fifty years, so I can't think why she'd be haunting the house."

No, I couldn't, either. Every once in a great while, a ghost would linger in a place simply because it was the site of too many happy memories for them to want to move on, but that sort of occurrence wasn't very common.

Still, since I didn't have much to go on, I figured I might as well try that angle.

"Do you know her name?" I asked.

"The daughter-in-law?" Nora responded. "Her name was Alice Bigelow. She passed away about six months after her husband. From all accounts, it was definitely a love match, no matter what anyone else said."

"'Anyone else'?" I said. Part of me felt vaguely guilty about indulging in such a gossipy conversation, but I tried to remind myself we were talking about people who'd been dead for nearly a hundred years.

"Oh, it sounded as though lots of people thought she married him for his money, but that simply wasn't true. Alice Cavendish came from a wealthy New York family and could have had her pick of anyone."

While that story sounded romantic enough, it didn't exactly help me to pinpoint the identity of the mansion's resident ghost. If Sam and Alice

Bigelow's marriage had been such a happy one, then there really wouldn't have been any reason for her spirit to keep hanging around there. No, she would have joyfully joined her husband in the afterlife.

Also, the girl I'd seen had appeared pale and tragic, definitely not a blooming bride. I didn't think Alice's specter would have presented in such a way, even if she'd decided to appear as her younger self, and not the mature woman she would have been when she passed away.

All in all, it didn't seem as if I was any closer to solving the mystery than I'd been before Nora called.

My disappointment must have been seeping right through the phone, because she added, "I'm sorry I can't give you any more information than that. But it's pretty much all I know."

"Oh, it's fine," I said hastily. "At least you've ruled out a couple of possibilities. I'll just keep poking around and see what I can find."

"Best of luck," Nora replied. "And congratulations!"

I gave her an absent thank-you before ending the call.

While I couldn't say it had exactly been a waste of time—it wasn't as though people had been beating down the door of the shop to pick up a new deck of Tarot cards or some incense—I still couldn't help feeling overwhelmed by a sense of futility. Whoever this ghost was, it appeared her connection to the house must be tenuous at best.

And that didn't make a whole lot of sense. Spirits always had a reason for haunting the places they lingered. I just hadn't been able to figure out this particular ghost's motivation yet.

But even though I tried to tell myself it was no big deal, and that I could take as long as I liked to discover her reasons for hanging out in the Bigelow mansion, part of me wasn't quite sure. What if she pulled another trick like the one with the chairs? The last thing I needed was to show up the day of the wedding and discover the pavilions had all been taken down and reassembled on the roof of the garage, or someone had dug a moat across the driveway, cutting off access to the property.

On the surface, those all sounded like some pretty wild ideas. However, I'd seen the way those chairs had been stacked…and I knew deep down in my gut that the party-supply guys hadn't been the ones responsible for the particular feat.

Something was telling me the ghost wanted to stop the wedding.

I needed to find out why.

7

Smudges and Spaghetti

BECAUSE IT WAS SO SLOW AT THE STORE... even though Friday afternoons were often busy for me...I went ahead and closed everything up at four, rationalizing that I wanted to go over to the Bigelow house and give it a thorough smudging and still have enough time to get back to my apartment and put together the spaghetti dinner I had planned for Calvin that night.

Besides, pretty much everyone in Globe knew I was getting married in a week, and so I didn't think anyone would complain too much about the shop having somewhat unpredictable hours between now and then. Yes, I possibly risked alienating a couple of tourists, but it wasn't the sort of thing that would keep me up at night.

I helped myself to some smudge sticks and an abalone bowl from the stock in the store, since I didn't feel like going upstairs and dealing with Archie's grousing about the way I closed down the shop every time some whim struck me. And all right, I did tend to get a bit capricious about locking up and heading out when I was busy following some clue or another, but in this case, I thought doing so was warranted. My main motivation was to attempt clearing the energies in the house, true, and yet I knew deep down I was hoping that the smudge ritual might draw out the ghost again.

As they say, nothing ventured.

The drive over only took me about ten minutes. As I pulled up, everything looked in order, no moats across the driveway, no trees uprooted and blocking the front walk.

And the rented chairs and tables remained blessedly in hiding inside the garage.

I shouldered my purse, now extra heavy because of the smudging supplies I'd stowed inside, and walked up to the front door, unlocked it, and let myself in. As before, the air was cool but not cold, and just the faintest hint of lemon furniture polish seemed to drift toward me.

Or was that lemon verbena?

A breath to steady myself, and then I went and set my purse down on the coffee table in the main salon. I pulled out the abalone bowl, a couple of smudge sticks, and a long-nosed lighter.

Time to get to work.

I lit one end of the smudge and held it over the bowl, waiting for the dried herbs to catch so I wouldn't have to worry about them going out as I walked from spot to spot inside the house. In my purse was also a small vial of sanctified salt, but I'd decided to hold off on that for now and wait to see how the smudge worked. I could only imagine the reaction of my mother's housekeeper if she came in to clean on Tuesday and found a faint line of salt in front of all the doors and windows.

Voice calm and clear, I said, "I command any negativity or non-benevolent beings within this space to leave and go to the light. You are not welcome here. I command you to leave and go to the light."

Walking slowly, I went from room to room, touching the smoldering smudge stick to corners and to doorway lintels, to window frames and even the banister of the mansion's grand staircase. Each time I paused and thought of the ritual words, murmuring them quietly as I put all my energy into an intention of protection and purity, ensuring that no negative energy would remain within the house.

"What on earth are you doing?"

There she was, standing in the front parlor, delicate features pulled into an expression of utter puzzlement. It was the first time I'd ever heard her utter a complete sentence, and I was kind of amazed at how human it made her sound. As before, she wore the same lacy white dress, although she seemed somehow more solid today, as if her confusion at my smudging ritual had managed to make her just a bit more corporeal.

"I'm smudging the house," I replied, doing my best to sound casual. Then again, this wasn't my first time holding a conversation with a ghost, although I had to admit that this young woman was about as different from Danny Ortega...or Lucien Dumond...as a person could be.

Her brow remained drawn together. "Whatever for?"

"It's a way of cleansing the energies in a place," I said. "A way of providing protection."

For a moment she was quiet, as if considering what I'd just told her. Then she asked, "Are you trying to cleanse *my* energies?"

Oh, boy. That was exactly what I'd been trying to do, but it didn't seem very diplomatic to come right out and tell my suddenly friendly ghost that. "Um...in a manner of speaking. That is, I just wanted to make sure everything was okay for when my family comes to visit next week."

"'Your family,'" she echoed softly. For just a moment, she looked almost wistful, as if thinking of the family she must have lost decades and decades earlier.

But then her chin went up, and her jaw hardened.

"Sometimes, family is a curse," she whispered, and, just as quickly, she disappeared. Less than a split-second later, a door upstairs slammed.

I winced. I couldn't see which door it was from where I stood, but I had a strong suspicion that had been the door to the front office.

Sometimes, family is a curse.

Whoever her family had been, clearly, they hadn't parted on good terms.

After that one door slam, however, the house became completely silent, except for the faintest hum from the A/C compressor outside. For a moment, I lingered where I stood, wondering if she was going to come back and resume our conversation. But as one quiet moment stretched after another, I realized our resident spirit didn't plan to reappear.

Frowning, I ground out the smudge stick in the abalone bowl, then went to retrieve my purse. It seemed I'd picked up one more data point… even if I had absolutely no idea what to do with it.

On the drive back to my apartment, I got out my phone on a whim and said, "Call Victoria Parrish." Obediently, the iPhone looked up the number and made the connection. A moment later, she answered.

"Hi, Selena. What do you need help with?"

"Oh, nothing," I replied. While I'd considered relating to my wedding planner what had just happened to me at the Bigelow mansion, I guessed that was a conversation better held in person. "I was just wondering if you'd like to come over to the apartment for dinner tonight. You haven't had a chance to meet Calvin yet, and I thought it might be a good idea for us all to get together."

A very brief pause, and then she said, "I would like to meet Calvin. But you're sure it's not an imposition?"

Considering that when I made spaghetti, I made enough for an army—I generally froze the leftover sauce for future quickie dinners—having Victoria over wouldn't be any trouble at all. "No, of course not," I reassured her. "Are you okay with spaghetti and salad?"

Her immediate response calmed my fears on that point. "It sounds great. I can't remember the last time I had a home-cooked meal—I mostly live on takeout and wedding food."

"Then you're definitely coming over," I said firmly. "Be at the apartment a little before seven, and I'll make sure you get a real meal."

A small laugh came through the phone's speaker. "Okay. See you at seven."

We ended the call there, and I tossed the phone back in my purse. Honestly, I wasn't quite sure what had prompted me to invite Victoria over, except she really did need to meet Calvin…

…and maybe I was thinking it would be a good idea for Archie to be around her a little bit more. For all I knew, familiarity would breed contempt, and he'd decide after listening to her chat at dinner that his strange attraction had been a momentary fancy and nothing more.

Okay, that was a pretty faint hope. But he'd also seemed so grouchy about me going to lunch with her and Hazel that I thought tonight's meal would be a bit of an olive branch. At least this way, he'd get to spend some time around Victoria that he hadn't even expected.

I didn't know whether he'd been spying or not, but as soon as I walked into the apartment, Archie lifted a furry eyebrow.

"So, where were you gallivanting this time?" he inquired sourly.

"I wasn't gallivanting," I replied in severe tones. "I was taking care of something at the Bigelow mansion." Pausing there, I sent the cat a speculative look. True, Jack and Alice Bigelow and their children were a bit before Archie's time, but maybe he'd heard something during his tenure in

Globe, a piece of gossip that had gotten lost over the intervening seventy years. "Did you ever hear of any kind of family trouble with the Bigelows?"

The cursed cat shot me a familiar look, the kind of glance that seemed to indicate he really thought I'd taken leave of my senses this time. "'Trouble'?" he repeated. "They were a very respectable family."

I supposed he would say that; the woman who'd interviewed him for his teaching position at Globe High had been Jack Bigelow's granddaughter. "Maybe so," I said carefully. "But sometimes families present a very different face to the world than they do at home."

Because this was such a patently true statement, there wasn't much Archie could say to rebut it. He lifted a paw, licked it, and then rubbed it against the side of his face. "I suppose so," he said grudgingly. "But I never heard even a whisper of scandal about the Bigelows. They hung on to the house until it got to be too much for the great-grandchildren, which was when it was sold to Hank and Nora Anders. Still, that sort of thing happens all the time."

"So, you never heard of a young woman dying there in the early 1920s?" I persisted. Maybe Archie really didn't have anything to tell me, but I didn't want to give up that easily.

Once again, he gave me one of those "candidate for the loony bin" stares. "No, I most certainly did not. Why would you even think such a thing?"

"Because the ghost I saw there was dressed like someone from around that time," I told him. "And she looks very young, like she was barely twenty or twenty-one when she passed away."

Archie made a noise that was half groan, half hiss. Over the past year, I'd learned that particular noise generally indicated he was annoyed with me, even if he couldn't come up with a precise argument as to why.

"I've never heard of anyone like that," he said. "And I don't know why you have to waste so much of your time talking to ghosts, especially now when you have much better things to do with your time."

He made it sound as if I was calling up the spirit hotline and chatting for hours at a stretch. "Ghosts often have important things to tell us," I returned. "And in this case, I want to know why she piled up the chairs for the reception in such an odd way."

"Possibly you should have asked her that first," Archie said, as if it should have been patently obvious.

Well, I supposed he had a point there. I'd been so startled that the ghost was speaking to me in something more than monosyllables, the thought hadn't even crossed my mind.

You know, I really hated it when my cursed cat was right.

"Next time," I said lightly, and then added before he could reply, "Oh, and Victoria's coming over for dinner tonight. You might want to get spruced up before she gets here."

Such a look of utter terror passed over Archie's face that I immediately felt bad for teasing him. Then he seemed to gather himself, expression turning bland.

"I'm sure it's utterly immaterial what I look like," he retorted. "But thank you for the warning."

After delivering that rejoinder, he turned and flounced out as only a cursed cat with a Virgo stellium could do. I had no doubt he was going into the office to sulk, but I decided to leave him be. My guests would be over in less than two hours, and I had a lot of work to do.

I'd texted Calvin to let him know Victoria would be joining us for dinner, and he'd responded with, *Great. Thanks for letting me know.*

Not the most effusive reply in the world, but he did tend to be concise in his texts, especially if things were busy at the station. It didn't sound as if they were working on anything big—and thank the Goddess for that…I didn't need murders or meth labs interfering, not when our wedding day was so close—but that didn't mean he and his deputies weren't still on the lookout for speeding tourists, trespassers, and the odd cow that had wandered out of its pasture and into someone's yard.

Anyway, that was why he wasn't surprised to see our wedding planner show up a few minutes before seven, and why he offered her a friendly greeting and a glass of wine almost as soon as she was in the door.

Somewhat to my surprise, she accepted. Maybe she hadn't wanted a margarita with lunch because she viewed that as work hours, but now that it was seven o'clock on a Friday night, a chianti was just what the doctor had ordered.

I called out a hello from the kitchen, where I was ladling sauce into a bowl and keeping a weather eye on the garlic bread, now just about ready to be pulled from the oven. Possibly some people might have thought it a little odd to be having such a hearty, warm meal when temperatures outside were just below ninety, but the air conditioning in my apartment worked great, and it wasn't as though I planned to spend all summer eating salad and gazpacho.

Soon enough, the three of us had sat down at the table. Out of the corner of my eye, I thought I saw Archie slinking into the living room and doing his best to occupy an unobtrusive spot so he could overhear everything we were saying without being too conspicuous. My mouth might have quirked a bit, but otherwise, I did my best not to draw any attention toward him. If he wanted to hang out and eavesdrop, that was his prerogative.

Once we'd dished up our food and clinked our glasses together in a toast to the success of Calvin's and my upcoming nuptials, my fiancé leaned back slightly in his chair and asked, "So, Victoria… what made you go into wedding planning?"

An innocuous enough question, one I'd wondered about myself. I was always curious about the paths people took that got them to where they currently were.

She'd been in the process of swirling some spaghetti around her fork, so she went ahead and popped the bite in her mouth, chewed, and swallowed before replying. "I've always liked being around beautiful things, I suppose," she said. "At first, I thought about being an interior designer. But I helped plan some parties in college, and then I helped my roommate out with her wedding because she really couldn't afford a planner, and I suppose it just clicked in my head that this was what I wanted to do. Less than a year later, I had my own company set up. It probably helped that I majored in business, so I knew what steps I needed to take to get started."

"That's impressive," I said. While I'd known from an early age exactly what I wanted to do—which was the reason why I'd dropped out of college partway through, since I knew no university degree could prepare me for a life as a professional psychic—I'd encountered plenty of people who hadn't known what they wanted to do with their lives until they were much older than their early twenties. "About how many weddings have you planned so far?"

Victoria smiled, although there was something almost rueful about the curve of her mouth. "Honestly? I don't have an exact count, but it's definitely in the hundreds by now. On busy months, I can be managing three or even four weddings at the same time."

"That's got to get crazy," Calvin said with a grin.

"It can," she replied. "But I love it. I can't think of anything more rewarding than giving couples the special day they've dreamed of." She paused there, still wearing that faint smile. "And I suppose you're both wondering why the wedding planner isn't married."

Calvin and I both made sounds of demurral, although I knew I was being a little bit disingenuous. Victoria wasn't wearing a wedding ring, and she certainly hadn't made it sound as though she was leaving a significant other behind to come stay here in Globe until the wedding, so I guessed she was unattached.

Whether or not my interest on the subject had anything to do with Archie's infatuation was a topic for a different discussion.

The laughing glint in Victoria's eyes told me she knew all too well what I'd been thinking... well, except for the part about my cursed cat.

"I was engaged," she went on after taking a sip of chianti. "But we both decided to end it—he wasn't on board with my crazy hours, and I needed someone who understood my work and would support me in it. My ex was just a little too clingy."

Well, then, it sounded to me as if Victoria and Archie were a match made in heaven. I'd never had any reason to try imagining what he'd be like as a romantic partner, and yet I had to believe he'd probably lose patience with anyone who was too needy.

This was all pie in the sky, of course, considering I didn't have any good leads on how to help him escape his feline existence.

"Sounds like a good move for everyone," Calvin said, his tone pleasant, almost neutral. Maybe he'd seen something in my expression, or maybe he was just doing his best to keep the conversation moving along.

"I think so," Victoria said lightly. She broke off a piece of garlic bread, and I took the cue to move the discussion in a different direction.

"I talked to the ghost again today."

Both Victoria and Calvin blinked at me, but she was the first to speak.

"You…talked to it? I mean, *really* talked?"

"Really talked," I agreed. "And the ghost is definitely a she. I still don't know anything about her—she didn't seem ready to volunteer much in the way of information—but it seems obvious enough to me that she had some kind of a beef with her family. Whether or not that has anything to do with why she's haunting the place, I don't know for sure. I have a lot more digging I need to do."

Calvin shot me a wary look, probably because he knew full well what I was like when I got the bit between my teeth. "Are you sure this is the right time for a paranormal investigation?"

"Yes," I said firmly. "I don't think she moved those chairs around just for kicks. I think she's trying to communicate something."

"You don't even know whether the ghost actually did that," he responded.

True enough. It wasn't as though I had a signed confession from the Bigelow mansion's resident specter telling me she'd stacked the chairs twenty high because she was bored and needed a diversion. At the same time, my gut instincts were pretty good…and they seemed to be sending a signal that I didn't have to look any further than the ghost when it came to the shenanigans with our rented tables and chairs.

"Let's just say I have a feeling," I said.

He smiled and shook his head, even as Victoria put in, "I've heard that your feelings are pretty accurate."

"A lot of the time," I replied. "I'm not saying my intuition is infallible or anything. But I'm really getting the impression there's a very real reason why the ghost has appeared and is causing mischief now, and if I can figure that out, then I'll have a much better chance of getting her to move on."

Victoria's clear blue eyes were bright with interest. "You can do that?" she asked. "Are you some kind of ghost whisperer?"

It was gratifying to see she was taking me seriously. Or maybe she was just trying to humor me because I was a client.

As soon as that thought passed through my mind, though, I immediately shot it down. She wasn't mocking me, but was genuinely curious.

"No," I said. "I mean, I might have helped a

couple of ghosts move on, but I'm mostly just your standard garden-variety psychic."

She grinned. "Is there really such a thing?"

"No," Calvin responded before I could reply. "Believe me, there's absolutely nothing garden-variety about Selena."

That remark made Victoria chuckle, and we went on to chat about Mavis Jones' Airbnb, Victoria's temporary digs in Globe—luckily, not the vacation rental where reality TV star Dillon James had met his end only a few months earlier—and about whether there would be any last-minute changes to the menu for the rehearsal dinner. I hoped it wouldn't be too same-y in terms of what we were serving at the reception, since the rehearsal dinner was being held at the Gold Dust casino's restaurant, but we hadn't had much choice in the matter. There really wasn't any place else in town where we could hold a sit-down dinner for fifteen people.

The evening wound down after that, and a little past eight-thirty, Victoria said goodbye and headed out. Calvin stayed to help me with clean-up, but he left soon afterward; he was scheduled to work early the next morning and therefore couldn't stay over.

Almost as soon as we'd kissed and Calvin had wished me a good night, Archie pounced.

"Are you doing this just to torture me?"

I turned away from the dining room table, where I'd been gathering the used napkins so I could put them in the hamper. "'Torture you'?" I echoed.

His tail swished back and forth in such annoyance that I wondered if it was going to detach itself completely from his body and go flying around the room. "By having Victoria come over for dinner."

Clearly, my little plan had backfired. Put on the defensive, I replied, "I would've thought you'd like having a chance to see her again."

Archie wrinkled his pink little nose. "So I could torment myself by hearing her voice, seeing her beautiful face, and knowing I'm stuck in this damned cat's body for all eternity?"

My cursed cat never swore, so his use of that word told me how shaken up he was. Remorse filled me, and I kept my tone gentle as I said, "I'm sorry about that, Archie. I suppose I was thinking that it would be worse for you to not see her at all. I didn't mean to upset you."

For a moment, he looked almost taken aback, as if he really hadn't been expecting an apology. His gaze wouldn't quite meet mine. Instead he seemed to find something terribly fascinating about the soft, smoke-gray fur on his paws.

Then he said, "I suppose I can see that." Another

moment of silence, one I guessed he was using to find the right words to say. "It's just...I never thought anything like this would happen to me."

I guessed he wasn't talking about being trapped in his feline form, but rather the entirely unexpected—and, I guessed, not entirely pleasant —sensation of finding himself drawn to another person in a romantic way.

"I understand," I said. "And I can make sure to meet Victoria at the Bigelow mansion or at Olamendi's or something if it really bothers you to have her come over."

A light of pure alarm entered Archie's golden eyes. "No, no," he replied hastily. "I can manage. I have to think she might ask questions if you suddenly changed the venue."

As best I could, I smothered a smile. He might have been acting noble, but I could tell he would rather be tormented by having her around rather than not get to see her at all.

"Oh, that's true," I said, my tone as serious as I could make it. "Then I'll just let things stand as they are."

"Good," he returned, humor somewhat restored now that he'd been assured I wouldn't be yanking Victoria Parrish out of his life. "You know how I hate change."

After delivering that pronouncement, he

disappeared back toward the office, where, I assumed, he planned to retire for the evening.

Now that he was gone, I allowed the smile I'd been holding back to spread across my lips. Archie might have tried to downplay the situation, but he obviously had it bad for my wedding planner.

The real trick would be figuring out how to solve his predicament.

8

Sign of the Cross

To my relief, Saturday was just busy enough at the store to justify keeping the place open all day, but otherwise, nothing much of note happened. I knew Victoria planned to be out of town for the day because she had a wedding to manage over in Tempe and wouldn't be back until late.

That meant Calvin and I could have a blissfully quiet evening at his place, barbecuing and enjoying steak and wine on the patio as the sun went down and the warm friendliness of an early-summer Arizona evening slipped around us. He had to work on Sunday—the price he was paying for taking ten days off starting on Thursday—but since he didn't have to be in until ten, that meant we could share a leisurely morning together before he headed in to work and I drove back to the apartment.

Despite my late appearance, Archie didn't utter a word of snark about my not being there right on time to feed him that Sunday morning. Of course, I'd put a generous helping of dry food in his bowl before I left the afternoon before, but that sort of responsible behavior hadn't exactly buffered me from his commentary in the past.

In fact, he seemed as though he was doing everything in his power to avoid me, as if he'd decided to be embarrassed about his outburst of the evening before and wanted to act as though it had never happened.

Well, if that was how he wanted to play it, I'd go along with him. The poor guy had enough to deal with as it was—I certainly didn't need to do anything to add to his embarrassment.

And although I was of half a mind to head back to the Bigelow mansion and see if I could try to pry more information out of the ghost, my instincts told me I needed to give her a little space, that she'd opened up to me on Friday afternoon, and putting too much pressure on her might cause her to disappear altogether…or worse, act out in a way that might not be as easy to repair as the problem of the stacked chairs had been.

Instead, I headed into my office—after taking

a quick peek inside to make sure Archie wasn't napping in there—and got out my Everyday Witch Tarot cards. Whether or not they'd be able to offer anything of value was the big question.

Well, as always, if the cards didn't give me the answers I needed, I could always reach out to Grandma Ellen in the crystal ball. We hadn't talked for a while, mostly because the run-up to the wedding had been hectic but hadn't involved anything that would have required her brand of otherworldly advice. I'd promised to show her all the photos from the wedding…at the same time wondering why she couldn't just peer in from her vantage point in the afterlife…and she'd wished me all the best and left it there.

All the same, I found myself wanting to hear the sound of her voice.

First things first, though. I lit the candles on the altar, including the special Road Opening one I'd been burning for the past month, figuring I could use the extra help to make sure the wedding went smoothly. After that, I sat quietly for a moment, letting the questions I needed answered resonate in my mind as I held the cards in my hands, allowing them to pick up the vibrations of my thoughts.

How can I discover the identity of the ghost haunting the Bigelow mansion?

I shuffled and shuffled, and shuffled a bit

more. A tingle in my fingertips told me it was time to stop, and so I paused and pulled the first card.

The Hanged Man.

Well, then.

To be fair, the card didn't *actually* mean someone had been hanged. No, its symbolism was more subtle than that, and generally indicated being stuck, or in limbo. And that phrase could definitely be used to describe the ghost who haunted the Bigelow mansion, not in this life or the next, but drifting somewhere in between. Usually a card pull wasn't quite so on the nose, but I decided to roll with it.

Up next…the Nine of Swords. Not exactly the cheeriest of cards, with a sad-faced witch sitting on a bed, so overwhelmed with grief and weariness that she couldn't even see the sun coming up outside her window. At its heart, though, it was a card that carried hope with it, in its symbolism of a new day and the realization that no one is as alone as they might feel.

The spirit at the Bigelow mansion certainly must have thought she was completely alone. I'd have to figure out a way to convince her that whatever might have happened to her in her former life, another one was waiting for her if she had the courage to reach out for it.

Frowning a little, I pulled the third card from the deck.

The Lovers.

I stared at it for a moment, not sure what to make of that one. Of course, the card had a literal meaning, of physical love, but it could mean much more than that. And in this particular situation, I honestly couldn't know for sure, not without a lot more information than I currently possessed.

Had my ghost been disappointed in love? Did she linger here because she'd died without being able to profess her feelings for someone?

Too often, it seemed as though every time I asked a question, I only got more of the same, rather than any concrete answers.

Doing my best to ignore the frustration mounting inside me, I shuffled the three cards back into the deck and then returned it to the green velvet pouch where my Tarot lived. I set the pouch on the bookshelf, then stared for a moment at the muffled shape of the crystal ball on the shelf below my Tarot collection.

Oh, well. Might as well go for broke.

I picked up the crystal ball and set it on my altar, careful not to disturb any of the candles burning around the perimeter. Just as carefully, I removed the embroidered cloth that covered it and put it down on the chair behind me. As usual, the crystal ball was absolutely clear, slightly distorting the objects behind it but not revealing anything of its true nature.

That was about to change.

"Grandma Ellen," I said, making sure each syllable was enunciated clearly and precisely. "I need to speak to you."

Nothing at first…but then a faint mist began to form inside the crystal, a mist that gradually resolved itself into the face of my late grandmother.

Of course, you wouldn't have known she was a grandmother just by looking at her, because she always materialized with the face she'd worn when she passed away at barely forty-two. It was some-times hard to gaze at her and realize that, as time wore on and she remained changeless on that other plane, I'd start to look older than she did.

But that day was still a decade off in the future, and for now, I had other things to worry about.

Her bright blue gaze fastened on me. "Hi, Selena," she said, as casual as if she'd just dropped in for a cup of coffee or something. "Aren't you supposed to be getting ready for your wedding?"

"I have been," I replied. It would be nice if people stopped asking me that question. I could manage my time just fine, thank you very much. "And I will be, when I run into something that has to be handled. Right now, though, I have a spare few minutes. I need to talk to you about the spirit at the Bigelow mansion."

For just a second or two, her image grew almost hazy, as though my grandmother had directed her energies elsewhere and so wasn't bothering to waste any additional effort on keeping her manifestation within the crystal ball sharp and clear. Then she nodded, as if she'd confirmed something to herself.

"A sad case," she said, and I found myself tensing.

"Sad?" I asked. "How?"

My grandmother's mouth compressed. "I'm afraid that's not my story to tell."

Great. This wasn't the first time Grandma Ellen had informed me she couldn't pass along the information I was so desperately seeking, but just because it had happened before didn't make me any less cranky.

"Well, she's messing with my wedding, and so I think I have a right to know what's going on," I retorted.

Grandma Ellen blinked. "'Messing'?" she repeated. "What do you mean?"

I briefly explained about the stacked chairs, and her brow creased a little before her expression relaxed into a smile that looked a bit too indulgent.

"That's just a prank," she said. "I don't see how that sort of thing could possibly stop you from getting married."

"Well, so far she hasn't caused too much of a hold-up," I said. "But who knows what she's going to try next? I'd rather be able to head her off at the pass, if you know what I mean."

My grandmother's smile faded, and the look she gave me next was almost stern. "That girl has seen more trouble and grief than you can imagine," she told me. "So, bear that in mind. There's no need to go rushing in with guns blazing."

"No one's guns are blazing," I snapped. "But I do think I should be able to get married in Mom's house without having to worry about everything going crazy the day of the wedding!"

At the mention of my mother, Grandma Ellen's expression grew gentler. "I wish I could be there with you two on your special day," she said softly. "All the same, it's the ghost's house just as much as it is your mother's. Don't create trouble where there isn't any."

After delivering that admonition, she faded away. I had to fight back the childish impulse to pick up the crystal ball and shake it. Like that would help. It wasn't a Magic 8 Ball; it wasn't going to shift and tell me, "All signs point to yes," just because I didn't like the first answer it had given me.

I fought back a sigh and picked up the ball, then returned it and its stand to their spot on the shelf, and draped the concealing embroidered cloth over the crystal.

My grandmother had said the house belonged as much to the ghost as it did to my mother. Was she speaking only of precedent—after all, the spirit must have been hanging around there for at least a hundred years, based on her clothing—or did Grandma Ellen truly mean the young woman had been a Bigelow?

But Jack and Alice Bigelow had had two sons, no daughters, a conundrum that only served to send me right back to the beginning.

When I got this frustrated, there was only one thing I could do.

I headed down the hallway to the kitchen and put on the kettle. What would calm my nerves most…Mystic Mint or Cozy Chamomile?

Decisions, decisions.

As I stood there, staring at the cupboard that held my tea collection, my phone rang. All too glad for the distraction, I hurried over to the dining room table and scrabbled around inside my purse, my fingers at last closing on the wallet case that protected my iPhone.

Nora Anders.

At once, I lifted the phone to my ear. "Hi, Nora," I said, telling myself not to get too excited even as my heartbeat began to speed up. Maybe she had some new information to divulge. "How are you?"

"I'm fine," she replied. "And I don't know if this will be of any help, but I was wracking my brains, trying to think of any information I might have overlooked, and I remembered that Alice Bigelow was a devout Catholic. In fact, she and Jack pretty much paid for St. Ignatius to be built there in town."

"Oh, really?" I asked. While it was an interesting detail, I couldn't quite see how this new piece of information would help me. Since I got the feeling Nora had expected me to be a bit more effusive about the fact she'd just relayed, I went on, "The church feels so old, I suppose I just thought it had been here longer than that."

Nora chuckled. "No, when Globe was booming as a mining town, there might have been some tent-revival preachers who came through here, but the only church at the time was a storefront rented by the Methodists. But I guess Alice got Jack to promise that he'd get a church built if she agreed to marry him and move to the wilds of Arizona, and so construction started on St. Ignatius almost as soon as she got here."

Again, this would all be interesting if I were writing a book on local history, but....

A sudden thought struck me. My grandmother had been pretty emphatic about the ghost belonging to the Bigelow house. If that was really true…if there actually had been a Bigelow daughter no one seemed to remember…then surely she must have been baptized at St. Ignatius.

And that meant the information about her birth date and her name might still exist somewhere in the church's records. They wrote all that stuff down when kids were baptized, didn't they?

Having never undergone the procedure myself, I couldn't say for sure. But it was definitely the best lead I had.

"Thanks so much, Nora," I said. "I think this is going to be really helpful."

"Oh, I hope so," she replied. "And that's the only other tidbit I could think of. But if anything else pops into my mind, I'll let you know."

I thanked her again, and we ended the call. As I set my phone down, I noted the time.

Two twenty-five.

Father Estevez held an afternoon mass at two o'clock every Sunday, which meant he was occupied at the moment. However, the service should be over in the next twenty minutes or so, and I knew that the priest tended to hang around a while afterward to tidy up and set everything in order after his parishioners had gone. If I timed this right, I should be able to catch him before he headed home to the modest little house he lived in a couple of blocks away from the church.

Archie appeared to still be hiding out in the laundry room, which meant I didn't have to worry about him asking what I was up to. I went into my bathroom, brushed my hair and refreshed my lip gloss, and decided I looked presentable enough to show up at the church. Father Estevez and I shared a sort of cautious regard for one another; I knew he didn't exactly approve of my pagan status, but at the same time, he respected me as an upstanding member of the local community. And while I certainly wasn't going to turn Catholic any time soon, I liked the priest very much, liked his quietly firm faith and the way he always seemed to be there for the people in his parish.

No messages from Calvin when I checked my phone one last time before I headed out. I hadn't really expected any, because he tended to maintain radio silence when he was at work unless we were trying to coordinate schedules or something important came up. All the same, I was glad that everything seemed quiet over at the San Ramon police station, because I wanted these last few days before the wedding to go as smoothly as possible.

Now all I had to do was figure out exactly what was going on with the Bigelow mansion's ghost.

Father Estevez looked surprised to see me when I approached him in the sanctuary, where he was picking up any hymnals left lying on the pews and returning them to their little racks on the seats in front of them. "Selena!" he said, straightening with a little difficulty. He appeared spry enough most of the time, but I knew he was pushing seventy-five, and more than once I'd wondered if he ever intended to retire.

Probably not. He seemed like one of those people who planned to drop in harness.

"What can I do for you?" he went on.

"I'm doing a little bit of a research project," I replied. As I'd walked over to the church, I'd decided it was probably better not to mention anything about the ghost, but make it sound as though I was just trying to look up a little local history. "I thought it would be nice to give my mother some background information on the Bigelow house and the people who built it, so I was wondering if your baptism records here go back that far."

If he thought it at all strange I was hunting down that sort of information when my wedding was less than a week away, he didn't give any sign of it. His expression turned thoughtful, and he gave me a pleasant smile.

"Actually, they do," he said, and a little wave of relief went through me. Maybe I really would be able to find what I was searching for. "I haven't looked at them, but Father Anselm—he was the priest at the parish here before he retired—told me they're all intact. In fact, I believe the Bigelow children were some of the first to be baptized here after the church was built."

That factoid seemed to line up with what Nora Anselm had told me. "Would you mind if I took a look at them?" I asked.

"No, not at all. But you won't be able to take them off the church grounds."

"Oh, that's fine," I assured Father Estevez. "I just want to take some notes."

"Then come this way."

He beckoned toward me, and I followed him out of the nave and into a hallway that seemed to lead to various meeting rooms and offices, as well as a kitchen for the times they hosted social functions here. This part of the building felt a lot newer than the chapel itself, and I guessed it had been added on to as necessary.

At the end of the hall was what appeared to be a small library, with shelves of books on all sides and several long tables in the center of the room. Father Estevez pointed at one of the chairs and said, "Go ahead and take a seat, and I'll see if I can find the baptismal register you're looking for."

I sat down and set my purse on the tabletop, then watched as he scanned several of the shelves, fingers moving along the leather-bound volumes until he finally stopped at one. After extracting it and taking a quick glance at the flyleaf, he went ahead and brought it over to the table where I was waiting.

"Here you go," he said. "This record covers the years 1899 through 1920. There are more after that, of course, but it sounded as if you were more interested in the earlier days of the Bigelows' tenure here."

"I am," I said, hoping some of my gratitude showed in my tone. "Thank you so much."

Father Estevez smiled. "It's no problem at all. I'm going to go back to the chapel and finish tidying up, so just come and find me there when you're done. You can leave the book on the table —I'll put it away."

Even better. It wasn't as though I planned to do anything even remotely illicit, and yet I still would have much preferred to check out the baptism records without the priest hovering over my shoulder.

"I will," I promised him, and he inclined his head toward me before heading back out to the hallway.

Now alone, I returned my attention to the book waiting on the table. Very gingerly, I opened the cover, which creaked faintly with the movement, as if it hadn't been looked at for years and years.

Well, probably it hadn't. When you came right down to it, there really wasn't a reason to check out baptism records like this, not when birth certificates served a similar function and were official to boot.

The first page of the book was inscribed in a spiky copperplate hand, *Baptismal Register for St. Ignatius, Globe, Arizona, 1899*. Those words seemed to indicate that the church must have been finished some time that year.

Which seemed to be the case, since the next page had a list of names, with various months and days progressing through that same year, starting in April—the month the church opened for business, so to speak. About halfway down that page was the entry I'd been looking for.

Samuel Christian Bigelow, August 20, 1899.

Only….

I bent closer to the page, squinting a bit as I stared down at the yellowed paper, at the somehow spidery copperplate handwriting. There was a weird grayish smudge below Samuel's entry, as if something had once been written there but had been erased by wetting the paper so the ink would run.

What in the world?

The lighting in the church's library wasn't all that great, so I picked up the book and went over to the window, where the bright sunlight from another blazingly blue day offered much better illumination.

Yes, that was a definite improvement. Even though the words were still smudged, I could catch just the faintest tracing of what they had once spelled out.

Susanna Caroline Bigelow, August 20, 1899.

Shock made my fingers tense around the book, and once more the binding creaked. Immediately, I released my grip, then took the volume back over to the table so I could set it down gently. A quick flip through the rest of the pages told me there were no more strange gaps like that, no odd smudges with blurred words underneath.

Samuel Bigelow had had a twin sister.

Had she died as an infant? That possible explanation didn't make much sense to me; if she'd perished young, as sadly happened all too often in those days, it still seemed as though people would have known about her, just as Josie had told me about Jack Bigelow's grandson dying of tuberculosis.

No, this seemed more as if someone had wanted to erase her very existence.

Why, though? If the ghost haunting the mansion actually was Susanna Bigelow—and my instincts told me that was exactly who she must be —then what had happened to cause her to remain in her former home for more than a century?

I didn't know. And I also didn't know whether she'd answer a direct question on the subject.

Still, I had to try. My gut was telling me that the only way to solve this mystery was to go back to the days before her death and try to reconstruct what had happened, what tragedy had forced her into this limbo. Maybe then I'd have the necessary insights to help her move on to the next plane… and to leave the house alone so Calvin and I could get married in peace.

After leaving the book on the table as Father Estevez had instructed, I took my purse and went down the hall back to the chapel, where he was just finishing putting away the last of the hymnals. He looked a little surprised to see me so soon, but all he said was, "Did you find what you were looking for?"

"I think so," I replied. "Thank you so much for letting me take a peek at those records."

"No problem at all," he said. "Come by any time."

Somehow, I didn't see regular visits to St. Ignatius in my future, but I had to admit Father Estevez had been very helpful. I sent him a friendly smile in response but didn't make any promises, and I could swear he almost winked at me.

We'd come to an understanding, the priest and I.

An exchange of goodbyes, and then I left the church, striding purposefully to the parking lot where my Volkswagen Beetle awaited me. I needed to get out to the Bigelow mansion, and right now.

I'd just have to wait and see how the ghost reacted when I called her by her name.

9

Call My Name

I STOOD IN THE FOYER OF THE MANSION, plotting my next move. Should I call out to Susanna here, or should I go upstairs, to the room I was sure had once been hers?

Probably better to go upstairs, even though it felt safer to remain down here in the foyer. If she reacted badly, I wouldn't have nearly as far to run.

But since acting like a coward wouldn't solve this particular mystery, I made myself walk up the steps and then turn to my right so I could follow the hallway that led to the front bedroom, now an office.

Oddly, unlike the other times I'd visited the mansion recently, I didn't sense any odd pressure in the air, didn't walk through any cold spots. The house felt curiously neutral, as though Susanna was occupied elsewhere.

Still, I was here, and so I had to try my best.

"Susanna?" I ventured. "Susanna Caroline Bigelow?"

Nothing. Oh, I detected the faintest hum from somewhere, as though the air conditioning had just kicked in after being dormant for a few minutes, but that was a completely ordinary sound.

"Susanna?"

Once again, only the hum of the A/C and nothing more.

Well, this was annoying.

I stalked down the hallway, calling Susanna's name at regular intervals. Even if I'd misinterpreted the entire situation and this ghost was no more Susanna Bigelow than I was, you'd think she'd appear to tell me to shut up so she could get some rest.

But the house remained stubbornly quiet, which meant that either she'd taken a powder or had simply decided to ignore me. That was the problem with ghosts; it could be extremely difficult to predict what they would do in any given situation, since their existences were so different from ours and they didn't have to play by the same rules.

Clearly, though, I wasn't accomplishing a darn thing here. No, if I wanted to find out more about what had happened to Susanna Bigelow, I was going to have to look elsewhere.

All right. If I couldn't get what I wanted straight from the horse's mouth, so to speak, I'd try something else. I needed to look at this like a detective…or at least, like a researcher.

The best source for learning more about Susanna Bigelow would be first-hand accounts of life in the town during the time period in question—diaries, letters, even articles from the local newspaper. Surely the death of a daughter of the town's leading citizens would be mentioned somewhere.

And that meant I probably needed to go to the library and see what it had in terms of a local archive of some sort.

Problem was, the library was closed on Sundays.

It's only a little setback, I told myself as I descended the stairs. *You still found a damn good piece of evidence today. Just open the shop late tomorrow and go to the library right when it opens, and see what you can dig up.*

With that plan settled, I let myself out, reengaged the deadbolt on the front door, and headed over to the spot where I'd parked my car in front of the detached garage. For just the briefest second, I thought I heard the sound of faint laughter drifting on the breeze, as if Susanna had been watching me the whole time and was highly amused by my futile attempts to reach out to her.

Laugh while you can, I thought grimly. *Because I'm getting to the bottom of this, one way or another.*

We'd planned to get together at Calvin's for dinner that night, and so while I was throwing together some quickie chicken tacos and rice, I told him all about what I'd found earlier that day.

"Have you ever heard of someone being erased from a baptismal register like that?" I asked. True, Calvin was no more Catholic than I, but I thought he might have some insights.

He scratched the back of his head, slightly mussing the sleek black ponytail he wore. I loved hanging out in the kitchen with him like this, sharing some wine during meal prep and discussing what had happened to us that day. Now, though, he just looked confused.

"I don't think so," he said. "I mean, I know I've read about people's names being stricken from the family Bible if they'd disgraced their relations for some reason, but an actual baptism record? That would mean the priest would have had to be doing the family's bidding."

I sipped some of my chenin blanc. "Well," I replied, "considering the family in question is the Bigelows, I don't think it's too strange that they might have been able to get the priest to do pretty much whatever they wanted. The question is, why on earth would they have done such a thing in the first place?"

Calvin's expression turned grim. "Well, if she'd brought shame on the family by getting pregnant out of wedlock or something like that, I suppose I could see why the Bigelows would have wanted to erase all mention of her."

This theory sounded plausible enough, if slightly horrifying. I had to remind myself that the mores of the 1920s were very different from those of the twenty-first century, and so I couldn't expect people back then to act in ways that seemed sensible to me.

"The ghost I saw didn't look pregnant," I said, my tone dubious. And yes, ghosts generally did have some control over how they appeared to us mortals, but still, if Susanna had died while carrying a child, she didn't show any physical signs of it.

Also, I had the feeling that something much more was going on here, something I couldn't quite pin down. I got the sense that maybe Susanna had upset her family in some way, only not in such an obvious manner.

"Then I don't know what to say," Calvin told me. He paused there, keen dark eyes searching my face. "You seem pretty wrapped up in this, Selena. Are you sure it's a good idea to be expending so much mental energy on solving this mystery when the wedding's only six days away?"

To the rational observer, it probably wasn't. Nothing in Calvin's tone told me he'd try to talk me out of solving this mystery, only that he was concerned about how much I was allowing myself to get scattered.

"I don't know," I said, realizing as I spoke that I sounded way too tired. "Honestly, until my mother and the rest of the gang show up on Wednesday, I don't have that much to do with myself. Maybe that's why I'm pushing now—I know I only have a few days left."

In response, Calvin came over, gently took the wine glass from my hand and set it on the counter, and then wrapped me in his arms. No words, just the silent reassurance that he would always be there for me.

And right then, it was enough.

The next morning, I slipped into the store, changed the "be back at" time on my little sign to eleven, and then headed over to the library. As with so many points of interest in Globe, it was only a few blocks away, and so I walked.

Just like the last time I'd visited, when I'd come here trying to find Danny Ortega's killer and thinking I might be able to unearth a clue in one of the high school's yearbooks, a member of the library staff was hoisting the American flag out front as I approached. I smiled at her and then headed inside, knowing I needed to go straight to the reference section toward the back of the building.

And the same stern-faced librarian with the iron-gray bob was working there, only now I knew her name was Barbara Tillman and that she sang in the Methodist church's choir. This time, since we'd gotten to know each other a little better over the intervening months, she even unbent enough to offer me a smile when I walked up to the reference desk.

"Hi, Selena," she said, her tone pleasant. "What can I do for you today?"

"Does the library have an archive of old letters, or diaries, or news articles from local sources?" I asked. "I'm looking specifically for stuff from 1899 to around 1920."

"That's quite a chunk of time," Barbara responded. "Would you like to narrow it down a bit?"

For a moment, I hesitated. I'd mentioned that

particular twenty-year span because it seemed most likely that whatever had happened to Susanna Bigelow, it would have occurred sometime within those two decades. However, since the ghost appeared to be in her early twenties at the very most, and I had to believe the incident in question had taken place sometime fairly close to the time she died, it made more sense to focus my energies there.

"Let's try 1919 to 1921 and see if I can find anything," I told her. Possibly, I was narrowing things down too much, but I reminded myself I didn't have unlimited time to play with. If this search didn't turn up anything, then I'd try expanding it later on and see what happened.

"The local archives are kept in a separate room," Barbara said. She extracted a set of keys from her desk drawer, then rose from her chair. "This way."

She led me past the stacks of reference books and to a door in the back wall of the building—or at least, what I'd thought was the back wall, although it didn't have any windows. After she opened the door, however, I saw that it revealed a small room with shelves on every side, and one round table in the center. On those shelves was a mishmash of books in various shapes and sizes, along with piles of manila folders that proved to contain letters, receipts, old flyers, and other ephemera. When I looked a little closer, I was relieved to see that the sections of each shelf were labeled by year, and so it shouldn't be too hard to drill down to the items I needed.

"The newspapers were too fragile to handle, so they were copied and bound into these books," Barbara said, pointing to a shelf where the volumes looked much more uniform and also bore labels indicating which year or years they covered. "I've been wanting to get them scanned and made into electronic files, but there just haven't been the resources available," she went on. "Years ago, they were supposed to be copied onto microfiche, but that didn't happen, either."

"The photocopies should be fine," I said quickly. To be perfectly honest, I didn't know whether the newspapers of the day would have even contained something scandalous about the Bigelows, considering the way that prominent family appeared to have controlled the town back then. Private letters or diaries felt like a safer bet.

But because the bound copies of the newspaper seemed a little easier to deal with, I figured I'd start there and then branch out as necessary.

"Come get me at my desk if you need anything," Barbara said, and then let herself out, leaving me alone with the rather motley collection.

I approached the shelf with the bound copies

of the local paper, then pulled down the ones for 1919, 1920, and 1921, and took them over to the table. Luckily, the Globe *Bugle* had been a weekly paper back then even as it was today, and so I didn't have to flip through hundreds of issues. In a way, it was fascinating to see what had dominated the local news at the time—births and deaths, disputes over land, the ups and downs at the mine.

Nowhere in there, however, did I see anything about the Bigelows, except as it related to their charitable works—the fund they set up for the families of the men who lost their lives in the mine, Alice Bigelow's contributions to the local Ladies' Aid society, that sort of thing.

There was even an announcement of Sam Bigelow's engagement to one Millicent Perkins, accompanied by a grainy photograph of the couple. Sam Bigelow looked tall and broad-shoul-dered, and had fair hair…just like Susanna, his twin.

If she was his twin at all.

I had to admit I sort of enjoyed catching this glimpse into Globe's history, even if it wasn't giving me any information at all about Susanna Bigelow. In all the accounts I read in those papers about the Bigelow family, there was never a single mention of a daughter. Sam's younger brother,

Joseph, even got a mention where it said he was leaving Globe to start a business in San Francisco…funded by daddy's money, no doubt. This piece of information lined up with what Josie had already told me, that one of the Bigelow sons had moved to San Francisco at some point, but that Samuel had stayed in his hometown and started a family.

Still, the newspapers weren't giving me what I needed, so I went and reshelved them, and then laid my hand on a manila folder of miscellanea from 1919.

No, my brain seemed to say. *Too early.*

Where that had come from, I didn't know. But my intuition often flared up in unexpected ways, and I'd learned to listen to it.

Similarly, I skipped over 1920 and went straight to 1921. Somehow, that felt better.

However, as I sifted through the collection of letters and recipes and receipts, I once again didn't see a single piece that made any mention of a Susanna Bigelow. I supposed I shouldn't be all that surprised; while it seemed to me that the reference staff at the Globe library had done a pretty good job of collecting what historic documents it could, this had to be a very small sample of what had actually been circulating at the time.

And I was all too aware of time ticking past as

I shuffled through folder after folder. I paused to pull my phone out of my purse to check the time and was startled to see that it was already a few minutes before eleven. Somehow, it didn't seem as though nearly an hour had passed as I delved into Globe's history, but clearly, I needed to pack it in.

I returned the folders to their place on the shelf, then slung my purse over my shoulder and headed back to the reference desk.

"Did you find what you were looking for?" Barbara asked, pausing in the middle of entering some information into her computer, maybe an interlibrary loan request or something like that.

"Not yet," I said, forcing myself to sound much more cheerful than I felt. "But I have some other avenues I need to try."

That statement bordered on an outright lie, because at that particular moment, I honestly had no idea where to start searching next. But since I didn't see the point in dragging Barbara into my current woes, I just thanked her and headed out. The store was waiting for me...even if I doubted any customers were.

The rest of the day passed without incident. Calvin had to work late, so I ate alone at the apartment, trying not to feel too put out that we couldn't spend the evening together. In fact, he was working the late shift all week until he went on leave after Thursday, which meant I was going to be left to my own devices a lot more in these days leading up to the wedding than I would have preferred. Not for the first time, I reminded myself that Calvin's job carried a lot more responsibility than mine, and that I needed to be a little more accommodating.

At least my mother, Tom, and his family would be arriving on Wednesday. Although I had to admit I really wasn't looking forward to dealing with Madison or Staci, we already had plans to all go out for dinner Wednesday evening after they got to town, so I figured I could slog my way through Monday and Tuesday, even deprived of Calvin's company as I was.

Archie was still acting subdued…for him… but I knew not to push things. He'd already been on edge, knowing that our quiet little life here at the apartment was going to come to an end in the very near future, and this whole situation with Victoria definitely wasn't helping. I could only hope that once the wedding was over and she'd headed back home to Scottsdale, he'd eventually be able to adjust to our new normal.

On Tuesday, I was mostly glad that I'd only

have to get through this last day at the store, and then I could devote all my energies to the wedding…and to the mystery of Susanna Bigelow and why her spirit lingered at the mansion. My research trip to the library had been a complete bust, and I didn't really know where to go from here.

That afternoon, my phone rang—my cell phone, and not the store's landline. This wasn't so unusual, because I'd already fielded calls from my mother, Hazel, and Victoria earlier that day, mostly to reassure them that yes, I wouldn't be at the store after this and they'd be able to get my undivided attention.

This call, though, wasn't from anyone in the wedding party. No, it was from Luisa Olvera, my mother's housekeeper.

A tingle of anxiety made its way down my spine, even as I told myself Luisa could be calling about something completely innocuous.

Still, this was the day she was cleaning the house in preparation for the arrival of my California relatives…which meant she'd been at the mansion all by herself.

"Hi, Luisa," I said after I swiped my phone's screen to accept the call. "What's up?"

"I didn't want to bother you this close to your wedding, Miss Selena," she said. Luisa always called me that; I had to wonder whether the practice would continue after I married Calvin, or whether she'd come up with some other way to address me. Her Guatemalan accent was still strong after more than thirty years in Globe, but her English was impeccable.

"It's fine," I assured her. "It's pretty quiet here at the store."

"Oh, good," she replied. "It's just that I'm not sure I can finish cleaning the house."

The tingle of anxiety morphed into an outright twinge. I almost didn't want to ask the question but forced it out anyway. "Why not?"

A small sound that might have been a sigh emanated from the phone's speaker. "You know I always start at the top of the house and work down, yes?"

"Yes," I said cautiously.

Another sigh. "Well, I noticed that some pieces seemed to be out of place, but I just put them back where they were supposed to be. I thought I could be imagining things—it's a big house, you know, and it has a lot of decoration."

That it did. My mother and Tom had bought the place with all the furnishings and bric-a-brac included, and so it was quite a bit fussier than her usual style of décor. More than once, she'd expressed her desire to declutter a little and remove the wallpaper, bring the house just a little more up to date, but so far they hadn't touched a thing.

And while I thought I had a very good idea as to who had been moving things around inside the house, I definitely didn't want to tell Luisa that. Susanna could be annoying, but she hadn't done anything that would actually hurt someone.

So far.

I made an affirmative sound, and Luisa clearly took that as a sign to continue.

"But when I got to the kitchen and was mopping the floor, the bucket tipped over and all the water spilled everywhere. I thought I had set the bucket down on something, and that was why it fell over, but nothing was there. And after I refilled it and put more soap in, the same thing happened." She stopped there and pulled in an audible breath. "I actually saw it fall over again. It looked almost as if someone had pushed it over, even though I was the only person in the house."

It seemed obvious enough to me that Susanna was up to her usual tricks, only this time she'd decided to torment the housekeeper, for whatever reason. Before I could say anything, however, Luisa continued.

"I've heard the stories, Miss Selena. I've heard how this house is supposed to be haunted. But I've been cleaning this place for almost a year now, and this is the first time I've ever had anything like this happen." Another of those pauses. "Is it haunted?"

Since she'd come out and asked me directly, I couldn't very well lie. "I think it is," I said. "But the ghost isn't malicious. She just likes playing practical jokes."

A murmur of something that sounded like, *Dios mio.* Then Luisa said, "I'm not sure if I can finish, Miss Selena."

Oh, no. If Luisa had made it to the ground floor, then that meant she'd already cleaned the majority of the house, including the all-important bedrooms and second-floor bathrooms. But we'd planned to use the bathroom on the first floor for the wedding, and people would be coming and going all over the place. If it was even a little less than spotless, I knew someone would notice…and maybe make a snotty comment that would land like a stink bomb in the middle of what was supposed to be a perfect day.

And forget about finding another cleaning service to finish what Luisa had started. They weren't exactly thick on the ground in Globe to begin with, and getting someone on this short notice would be nearly impossible.

"It will be fine," I said in a rush. "Just hold tight, and I'll be right over."

"What are you going to do?"

"Whatever I have to," I said grimly.

Trying to ignore the sensation of inevitability that threatened to overwhelm me, I locked up the store and put the sign in the window, the prettily lettered one that I'd made up and had laminated, letting everyone know that Once in a Blue Moon would be closed until Monday, June thirteenth. It felt wrong to bail out at three-thirty when the shop was going to be shuttered for the next ten days, but I didn't have much of a choice.

I had to contend with a little after-school traffic on my way over to the mansion, but soon enough, I was pulling up into the driveway. Luisa's older-model but meticulously maintained Ford Explorer was parked in front of the garage, and so I left my Beetle next to it before shouldering my purse and heading up the front walk.

Luisa was sitting on one of the benches on the porch, her brows knitted in worry. Just like every other time I'd seen her, she wore a blue smock over faded jeans and a T-shirt, and her gray-shot dark hair had been pulled back into a ponytail. Her expression brightened as soon as she saw me, however, and she stood up when I mounted the porch steps.

"Thank you for coming," she said.

"It's no problem," I assured her. And okay, it kind of was, but I needed to make sure the house was clean and ready for its guests. If worse came to worst, I'd finish the task myself, but I knew I wouldn't be able to do nearly as professional a job. "Why don't you wait out here, and I'll go inside and see if I can figure out what's going on."

Luisa's plump features appeared almost comically relieved at this offer, but at the same time, she seemed to hesitate. "Are you sure, Miss Selena? I don't know if you should go in there by yourself."

"Don't worry," I said. "This ghost and I are old friends."

Having delivered that remark, I turned the knob and went inside. The house smelled of lemon and beeswax, although this time I was pretty sure those scents were the product of Luisa's cleaning efforts and not Susanna Bigelow's signature perfume.

And unlike the last time I'd visited, I sensed that pressure on my chest almost right away, signaling the ghost had to be lurking somewhere nearby.

"Susanna!" I called out. "I know you're here. You've been messing with poor Luisa, haven't you?"

No response…not that I'd been expecting one right away.

I huffed out an exasperated breath and said, "I can do this all day, you know. My shop's closed until after the wedding, and so I don't have anything better to do than hang out here."

Another of those silences, but then Susanna Bigelow materialized a few feet away from me. As before, she had on the lacy white tea-party dress, but her face wore a thunderous scowl.

"I don't see why I can't have some fun," she said.

"Because that 'fun' is at the expense of a hard-working woman," I responded calmly. While I would have dearly liked to tell Susanna she was acting like an utter brat, I thought the diplomatic approach would better serve me here. "And also, Luisa's been here to clean plenty of times before, and you never gave her a hard time then. What's the problem now?"

Susanna's pretty mouth pushed into a pout. "I don't want those people coming here."

"Which people?" I asked. "My family?" To be honest, I could kind of understand Susanna not wanting Tom's family under her roof, because they annoyed the heck out of me as well. However, since this would be their first visit, I had to guess her opposition on this particular occasion didn't have anything at all to do with the actual people involved.

"All of them," Susanna replied, with a sweep

of her hand as if to indicate the grounds of the house as a whole.

Understanding struck. It wasn't Tom's kids, as difficult as they could be to deal with. No, Susanna just didn't want *anyone* coming here for the wedding.

"Is it because it's for a wedding?" I asked next.

Under the lacy dress, her small chest heaved. "If I couldn't get married here, then no one will!"

And she stamped her foot in its delicate beige kid Mary Jane shoe, then promptly disappeared.

Well, that put a different spin on things. As long as the home's visitors were simply Airbnb guests, she couldn't have cared less, and had left them alone. Now that a wedding was being planned on the premises, however….

What had happened to her to make her so bitter on the subject?

I had to guess that her parents must have intervened to keep her from making an unsuitable match, although that theory still didn't explain why she was haunting the place, or why every mention of her seemed to have been erased from existence.

And it also didn't help me with my current predicament. Somehow, I had to keep her from interfering with the wedding. It was far too late in the game to even consider moving to another venue, and so I needed to figure out a way to make sure everything would run smoothly without any ghostly interference.

Well, I could try purifying the house again. True, that hadn't worked so well the first time, but I'd brought palo santo with me today, thinking its stronger energies might have an effect on Susanna when simple smudging hadn't. I hardly used the rare wood anymore, since it was being over-harvested and offered its own set of issues—I tried to avoid cultural appropriation whenever possible —and yet every once in a while, I'd dip into my stash when the situation was dire enough.

Doing my best to hold an image in my mind of the house clear and unbothered by any negative energies, I lit the wood in an abalone bowl and walked from room to room, summoning all the positivity I could muster, while at the same time wishing for Susanna to have a peaceful afterlife, and to move on from whatever hurts she might have suffered while still alive.

When I returned to the front salon, however, it was to find her standing there with her arms crossed, an almost snotty expression of amuse-ment on her delicate features.

"Did you really think that was going to work?" she inquired.

Well, I'd hoped it would. Anger bubbled up in me, even as I forced myself to say in the calmest tones I could muster, "Generally, it does."

"There is nothing 'general' about this situation," she replied.

"Maybe not," I allowed. "But you need to understand that I'm getting married to Calvin Standingbear here on Saturday, and nothing's going to stop that."

Her mouth quirked. "If you say so."

"I do say," I said, a little surprised I was holding it together so well. Then again, experience had taught me that losing my temper generally didn't accomplish very much. A sudden idea occurred to me, and I added, "And maybe my smudging isn't doing what I'd like it to, but we can always see what would happen if I had Father Estevez come up here to perform an exorcism."

Ghosts couldn't exactly go pale, but I could tell from the way Susanna's expression fell that she didn't like that threat at all. I honestly had no idea whether the priest would even perform such a ceremony, and yet I hoped the threat of bringing in some churchy big guns might make Susanna, who must have been raised Catholic, have second thoughts about the holy hell she'd been raising at the Bigelow mansion.

Rather than respond directly, however, she just disappeared. At the same time, the pressure I'd felt on my chest and throat eased, telling me she really was gone and not simply lurking around the house somewhere.

Only time would tell whether this was a temporary victory or not, but for the moment, I'd take it.

I opened the door, and smiled out at Luisa.

"It's safe to come in."

10

Luck of the Draw

OBVIOUSLY, I RELATED NONE OF MY interactions with Susanna the ghost to my mother. No, I just sent her a text saying that the house would be in perfect shape when they arrived the next day, and she messaged back saying she was tremendously excited and couldn't wait to see me.

For just a moment, I couldn't quite hold back a flicker of resentment toward Susanna Bigelow. I should've been allowing myself to get as excited about the upcoming wedding as my mother and everyone else in the family, but instead I was spending all my energy trying to discover what had happened with the ghost and why she seemed so dead set on preventing my wedding.

However, I did have a date with Victoria to go over to Globe's tiny little bridal salon to pick up my gown. Since Calvin would be working late, I knew there wasn't the slightest risk of him seeing the dress when I brought it home, so the timing worked out perfectly.

And even though my mother had expressed her doubts when I'd told her I was going to shop local for my bridal gown rather than going into Phoenix, I knew I'd made the right choice as soon as Thora, the shop owner, brought out the dress and I tried it on to make sure no last-minute alterations were needed. It was simple enough in style, all-over lace with a deep V of a neckline and gorgeous lace flutter sleeves I could detach for the reception, and it suited me so much better than anything structured or poufy.

"Oh, it's wonderful," Victoria said as I stood on the little dais Thora used for alterations. "So utterly you."

I'd thought the same thing, but it was nice to have that opinion corroborated by an expert. And I had to give kudos to Thora, who'd taken my input all those months back and had helped me select a dress that was perfect for me.

"Thank you," I said as Thora slowly circled the dais, eyeing the gown critically to make sure it fell just so and didn't bunch or pull anywhere.

Apparently, it passed muster, because she came back around and finally allowed herself to smile. She was probably around my mother's age, but almost severe in appearance, with dark hair she always wore back in a twist and deep red lipstick on her wide mouth. I didn't think I'd ever seen her wear anything but black, and had wondered more than once if she'd adopted that somber palette so she wouldn't steal attention from the gowns she sold.

"Yes, it's lovely," she said. "And the headpiece."

She lifted the simple crown of silk flowers I'd chosen to complement the gown and set it on my head. From the beginning, I'd known I didn't want a big veil or a tiara or anything like that, and again, the little flowered headpiece felt just right. Of course, it would look much better when my hair was styled to go with it, but still, I got a pretty good idea of what the end result should be.

Once again, Victoria nodded in approval. "Just the perfect touch. And no alterations?" she added, glancing over at Thora.

"No, it's ready to go," she said. "Selena, you can take it with you today."

Which was what I'd planned, but still, it was nice to get confirmation from the shop owner that I wouldn't have to do anything else to the gown. I went back to the dressing room, carefully extricated myself from the dress, and then handed it and the floral crown over to Thora so she could bag it all up. There probably wasn't much chance of Calvin getting a peek at my bridal ensemble, since we didn't have any plans for him to stay at the apartment this week, but I was going to hang it in the office closet anyway, just to be safe. The wardrobe I'd purchased for Archie from a bunch of online stores a few months back occupied the same space, although I knew there was still room at one end for the wedding gown.

Thinking of Archie's clothes sent a flicker of sadness through me. Back when I'd bought them, I'd hoped that putting the intention out into the universe of returning him to his human form might help the situation, but so far, absolutely nothing had changed.

Well, except for his improbable infatuation with Victoria Parrish.

We finished up at the bridal shop and went our separate ways. For just a moment, I'd wondered whether I should invite Victoria back to the apartment so we could get takeout or something, but then I decided against it. After dealing with the continuing drama at the Bigelow mansion, I just wanted a quiet evening at home with my cursed cat.

It would be one of the last times Archie and I could share time like this together, what with the relatives arriving the next day and then all us girls heading out to Gilbert on Thursday to spend the day getting pampered at a spa before having dinner together. Early on, I'd put my foot down about a bachelorette party, since the whole notion seemed pretty silly to me, but we'd compromised by agreeing to a spa day together. At any rate, I wouldn't be home Wednesday night, since Calvin and I were going out to eat with the family then, and with Thursday occupied in Gilbert and Friday being spent on the rehearsal dinner, poor Archie was probably going to be feeling somewhat neglected.

I'd bought all his favorite treats, though, and I planned to get takeout chicken fajitas for dinner that night, since I knew he had a weakness for them. And I had to admit that he did seem slightly more relaxed when I came in with my bag of Mexican food, probably because he knew we'd be able to share it without getting interrupted.

And because I'd already made a mental vow not to bring up the wedding or the current madness going on at the Bigelow mansion, we did manage to have a nice evening, with both of us on our best behavior. Not once did he bring up his apparently unending feline state, even though he must have given up at that point, with the wedding now less than four days away.

It did feel odd to wake up Wednesday morning and realize that I wouldn't be going into the shop, that it was now officially shut down until Calvin and I got back from our honeymoon. However, we'd already agreed to meet for lunch at one o'clock, since dinner was off the table thanks to his work schedule.

Almost as soon as he sat down across from me at The Flatiron, however, my phone buzzed.

I shot him an apologetic look. "Sorry," I said as I extricated the iPhone from my purse and glanced down at the screen. "I need to take this— it's my mom."

"No worries," he replied, sending me one of those wide, warm smiles I loved so much.

And he picked up the menu and began to peruse it, although—just as with every other local restaurant we frequented—he'd probably memorized everything on it long ago.

To be honest, I'd been starting to get a little worried about the radio silence from my mother. She'd told me that they'd all planned to get on the road a little after ten, which would have put the caravan in Globe somewhere between five and six, depending on how long they stopped for lunch. But here it was one, and I hadn't heard a single thing.

Well, I was hearing now.

"Hi, Mom," I said. "What's up?"

"Not much," she replied. Her usually sunny tone sounded downright annoyed. "Madison and Tony just now showed up at the house. Nick and Staci were late, too, but not like this. Anyway, there's no way in the world we're going to make it to Globe in time for dinner, so we're going to have to cancel."

"Oh, I'm sorry," I said, even as I thought the whole situation was classic Madison. Honestly, I didn't think that woman had been on time for her own birth. Probably, my mother had been overoptimistic in thinking the couple would make it to the house in the Valley for a 10 a.m. departure, but maybe she'd hoped that even if her daughter-in-law was running late, they'd only be off by forty-five minutes or so. I had to admit that being three hours late was pushing it even for her. "What happened?"

"Madison happened, that's what," my mother replied, although her voice dropped a little, as though to make sure no one could overhear what she was saying. In the background, there was a bustle of activity and voices, and so I guessed she'd slipped away to make a quick call before they all got on the road.

"Well, that's okay," I said, doing my best to sound cheerful and unconcerned. "I mean, we girls are all going out together tomorrow, and then there's the rehearsal dinner on Friday, so it's not as if we're not going to be socializing a whole bunch."

"True, but still…." She let the words trail off, and although I couldn't see her, I had a feeling she'd given a resigned lift of her shoulders. It was pretty hard for my mother to stay angry with anyone for too long. "Anyway, I just wanted to let you know."

"Okay. Text me when you get in."

"It's going to be pretty late."

"That's all right," I assured her. "I should still be up." For a second or two, I wondered if I should warn her about the ghost, then decided to let it go. After that threat about bringing in Father Estevez, Susanna had gone quiescent…for the moment, anyway. Luisa had finished the rest of the housecleaning without any issues, but to be safe, I'd gone over to the house this morning and left a protection spell jar in the upstairs office that probably had once been Susanna's bedroom. Maybe it would work and maybe it wouldn't, although I had to hope the ghost had learned her lesson and would leave things alone.

Otherwise, my wedding would definitely end up being a memorable one…although not in the way I'd intended.

"Then I'll text you later," my mother told me. "Take care, and send our love to Calvin."

"I will." I ended the call and put the phone back in my purse.

"Everything all right?" he asked.

I let out a sigh and reached for the glass of ice water Ingrid, the restaurant's owner and occasional waitress, had left on the table for me. "Oh, mostly," I said. "They're running late because Madison is up to her usual shenanigans, so we won't be meeting for dinner."

He didn't quite roll his eyes, but I could tell by the shift in his expression that he wasn't exactly looking forward to meeting his future step-in-laws. However, he apparently decided it was better not to comment on that subject, and instead said, "I wish I didn't have to work late tonight."

"It's fine," I replied. "I'll just have a quiet evening with Archie. It's probably better this way. Things are going to be pretty hectic the next few days."

"True." Calvin reached across the table and took my hand, then gave it a reassuring squeeze. "Hanging in there okay?"

I managed a smile. "Sure. And just think— this time next week, we'll be sipping chardonnay in Sonoma."

He smiled back at me, dark eyes lighting up. "Definitely something to look forward to."

Ingrid came by to ask what we wanted to eat, and we chitchatted a bit about the upcoming wedding before she headed back to put in our food order with the kitchen. I let myself relax a little, thinking it was good that Calvin and I had been able to steal this time together, that I'd actually been given a little grace before the relatives descended and everything kicked into high gear.

Who knows? Maybe with a little extra peace and quiet at home this evening, I'd be able to figure out what really had happened to Susanna Bigelow…and how to get her out of the mansion before the big day arrived.

Well, a girl could hope.

Later that afternoon, however, after getting only minor arcana mishmash from my Tarot cards, and absolutely nothing from the pendulum or the little bag of runes I only pulled out when I was feeling particularly desperate, it felt clear enough to me this wasn't the day for inspiration to strike. It seemed pretty obvious that Susanna had been frustrated in love, but I couldn't really come up with anything more concrete than that basic hypothesis.

And as much as I'd embraced the idea of having another quiet evening alone, I didn't know whether I was up for one after all. I almost thought of calling Hazel to come over, but it didn't seem right to ask her to give up an evening with Chuck just because I was feeling edgy and needed someone to talk to.

Then I thought, *Why not call Victoria?*

Maybe that was asking a bit much of Archie, but, on the other hand, he'd seemed pretty downcast when I'd told him that morning that I didn't think the wedding planner would have any further reasons to visit my apartment. At this point, all the action was moving to the Bigelow mansion.

But Victoria would be home alone this evening, too. While I had to believe she must have plenty of things to keep her occupied—seriously, I didn't think she ever took a real break from work —it didn't seem too out of line to invite her over so we could discuss any last-minute changes or things to look out for as the big day loomed ever closer.

The more I thought about it, the better the idea seemed. However, I knew I needed to run it by Archie, just to be sure.

He wasn't in the laundry room on his beloved rug, and so I headed out to the main living area. Sure enough, there he was, lying in the middle of the sofa. Although he looked asleep, I knew better.

Proving my point, he cracked an eyelid as soon as I entered the room. "What?" he asked.

He sounded grouchy, but since that was his normal state of being, I wouldn't allow his gruff tone to stop me. "I was thinking about having Victoria over for dinner tonight," I said. "Calvin's working, and I thought it would be nice to have some company. Is that okay with you?"

In response, he stretched out on the sofa cushion, looking as though he didn't have a care in the world.

I knew better, though.

"If you must," he replied at length, tone one of such extreme *ennui* that I understood immediately he'd be all too happy to see Victoria once more, even if he did end up complaining about being "tortured" again.

"Great," I said cheerily. "Then I'll text her and see if she's free."

Knowing I had the cat's tacit permission, I went over to the dining room table and got out my phone, then sent a quick text.

Hey, Victoria. I was wondering if you'd like to come over for dinner? Nothing fancy, but I thought it might be nice to chat.

I didn't get a response at first, which worried me. What if she was formulating a polite way to decline? Maybe she thought it a little strange for me to be inviting her over for dinner when there was no real reason to do so.

A moment later, though, my phone pinged.

You're sure it won't be too much trouble?

Not at all, I wrote back. *I thought I'd make some asian chicken salad, if that works for you. I make a mean sesame dressing.*

Sounds great, she responded. *What time?*

How about six-thirty? I have a big day tomorrow, so I don't want things to go too late.

That works. I'll see you then.

With that settled, I put down my phone and called out to Archie, "She'll be over at six-thirty."

"Wonderful," he grumbled, and curled up into a ball, his back to me.

If he wanted to play it cool, fine. I could tell he was excited…and I was excited on his behalf.

First, though, I needed to do some shopping, which should help to fill up the rest of the afternoon. I supposed I could have headed out to the Bigelow mansion to see if Susanna was up to any mischief, but she'd seemed pretty cowed after that threat about Father Estevez, and so I decided it was better to let it lie for now.

Anyway, I had a dinner to prepare.

Victoria showed up at six-thirty on the dot, which I supposed was only appropriate for someone whose entire professional life revolved around schedules and making sure everything happened precisely when it was supposed to happen. She wore yet another of her sheath dresses, this one in a pretty shade of sage green, and held a bottle of chardonnay.

"I thought it would go well with the chicken salad," she said, handing the bottle to me as she entered the apartment.

"It'll be great," I told her. "Go ahead and sit down—I just need to bring out the salad and the bread."

She nodded and took one of the seats at the dining room table where I'd put out a place setting, and I set down the wine before heading back into the kitchen. I had some pinot grigio in the fridge, but the chardonnay would do just as well.

A few minutes later, we both had bowls heaped with chicken salad and glasses full of chardonnay. I couldn't help noticing how Archie had lain down at the edge of the living room rug, far enough away that he appeared disconnected from what was going on at the dining table, even though I knew he must be listening to every single word.

"Have you heard from your mother?" Victoria asked after we'd both taken our obligatory first sip of wine.

I'd texted Victoria earlier that day to let her know the wedding party was coming into town late, so she was familiar with my mother's tale of woe. "She sent me a text when they stopped in Palm Springs for an early dinner," I said. "It looks like they'll be pulling into Globe around nine or so."

"Well, at least they're getting here today," Victoria replied, obviously doing her best to be diplomatic. I actually hadn't said word one to her about the way Tom's daughter Madison got on my nerves, but I had to believe someone as punctual as my wedding planner didn't have much use for anyone who could run that late for something as important as a wedding.

"Right," I said, figuring I'd take my cue from Victoria and try to be as diplomatic as possible. "And it won't be hideously late, either, so they should be able to get a decent night's sleep."

"And what are the guys going to do while you're off in Gilbert?" she asked.

"Oh, it sounds like they're going to head up to Payson to play golf," I said. This plan was Tom's, obviously; the man loved to golf. And Calvin was going along with it because he loved me to death, and not because he had any desire to spend his Thursday out on the links with my stepfather and his son and son-in-law. I'd heard Calvin's father Raymond had been invited along on the outing, but he, smart man, had manufactured some sort of plausible excuse to avoid the excursion. The two of us might have had a rough start, but now Raymond and I definitely had formed a mutual admiration society.

Victoria gave an approving sort of nod, which seemed to signal to me that this was a normal way for the men in a wedding party to spend some sort of bonding time together. I didn't know how much bonding would actually go on; Calvin and Tom got along great, but since Tom's son Nick and Madison's husband Tony weren't exactly the sort of people my fiancé would choose to hang out with, I had a feeling he'd be polite and not much more.

At least it would get them out of the house for a few hours.

"And what about you?" I asked. "Do you need to head into Phoenix for work?"

"No," Victoria replied, and I found myself relaxing a bit. Yes, I was going to be otherwise occupied pretty much all of Thursday, but I still felt safer knowing she planned to remain in Globe. "My next wedding isn't until the eighteenth, and so I know I'll be on the phone a lot, but there's nothing going on that can't wait until next week."

I nodded and helped myself to another forkful of chicken salad. As I chewed, an idea popped into my head. Maybe a slightly underhanded idea, but….

"Could you do me a favor, then?" I asked, and immediately Victoria tilted her head toward me.

"Sure," she said without hesitation. "What do you need?"

"Since we're going to be in Gilbert kind of late, I won't be here to feed Archie his dinner," I told her. "Would you mind swinging by and giving him his food, checking his water? He usually eats sometime between six and six-thirty."

At the mention of his name, Archie gave up all pretext of sleeping and glared at me with a pair of baleful golden eyes. Luckily, Victoria had her back to him, so she was blissfully unaware of his reaction to my suggestion.

"No problem," she said. "I was thinking about coming here to Broad Street to get a sandwich from Cloud Coffee for dinner, so I can come by and feed Archie then."

Well, that seemed to be settled. And I had to admit I was cheered by the way Victoria had said his name and not just "the cat." Obviously, she wanted to make sure he felt included and cared for, even if she could have absolutely no idea of the actual truth about his identity.

"Great," I replied. "I'll give you a spare key to the building's back door and to the apartment before you leave. And I just won't turn on the alarm tomorrow."

"Sounds like a plan."

We talked a little bit about the wedding—how the pavilions and the occasional furniture were going to be delivered Friday morning and set up then, how the weather looked as though it was actually going to cooperate, with temperatures dropping out of the low nineties and into some much more comfortable mid-eighties—and then the conversation lulled a bit as we returned to our salads and I poured Victoria some more wine.

As we'd spoken, I'd noticed just the tiniest bit of weariness come and go in her expression, disappearing so quickly that I wondered if I'd imagined it. Still, the wine I'd drunk during dinner made me a little less cautious.

"Does it ever get exhausting?" I asked. "Managing all these moving pieces all the time, I mean."

At once, Victoria sat up a little straighter, and she put on a smile that looked genuine enough, even though I thought I knew better. "Oh, no, I love my job," she said. "I don't want you to think I'm tired of it."

"That's not what I said," I replied. "And it's okay—we're friends here. You can let down your hair if you want."

She chuckled at that comment, probably because so far, I'd never seen her with her hair in anything other than that sleek twist which made her look quietly professional. Behind her, Archie gazed intently in her direction, as though he, too, wanted to know the answer to my question.

"Okay," she said, still smiling a bit. "Sometimes it can be kind of a lot—the hours are crazy, and you never know when you're going to get a hysterical bride texting you at 2 a.m. because the wedding's in three days and she's decided she hates the flowers. Not that you would do anything like that," she added hastily.

No, I probably wouldn't. While I wanted the wedding day to go as smoothly as possible, the most important thing was to get married to Calvin and make sure our guests had a good time. If a few mishaps occurred that would make us laugh about the whole thing later, that was all right by me.

"That sort of thing would drive me up a tree," I said frankly, and she laughed again.

"I think being a wedding planner requires a certain kind of temperament, that's for sure." Her expression grew more serious, and she sipped some chardonnay before continuing. "Lately, I've been wondering whether I should take a break, go back to school to get my interior design certification after all. It can be demanding, because you're working with clients to make their homes or places of business beautiful, but it's still not quite as high-pressure as planning a wedding."

"No, probably not," I agreed. "Well, if you do decide to make a change, I'm honored that I got to be one of your wedding clients."

She shook her head. "Oh, I'm not making any immediate plans to hang up my hat. It's more just…thinking."

A thought occurred to me. "Why don't we see

if you're on the right track?" I asked. "I can do a Tarot spread for you."

"You really don't need to do that—" Victoria began, now looking vaguely alarmed.

"No, I want to," I said. "You can believe it— or not believe it, if it's not really your thing. But the cards really are good at providing some guidance."

Since she didn't offer any other protests—and because we were almost done with dinner anyway —I went into the office and got out my Everyday Witch Tarot, then headed back to the dining room. In my absence, Archie had retreated to the couch, probably because he wanted to make sure there wasn't any chance of Victoria noticing that he'd been eavesdropping on our entire conversation.

"Any more salad?" I asked as I returned to the table, and she shook her head.

"No, thank you. It was wonderful, but I'm full now."

As was I. The salad was surprisingly filling, especially when paired with some fresh-baked bread and butter.

"Then I'll go ahead and clear the table, give us some space."

She made a movement as if to help, but since there really wasn't a lot to pick up, I told her I'd take care of it. A moment later, the table was cleared of everything except our wine glasses, and I sat back down again and started shuffling the cards.

"You don't have to tell me the question you're asking," I told Victoria. "Just hold it in your mind, and the cards will pick up on your vibrations."

One corner of her mouth lifted. "Well, you already know the question. Is a change of career in the cards for me?"

I couldn't help smiling a little at that particular phrase, but I kept shuffling until the cards felt right. Then I laid the first one on the table.

The Ace of Pentacles. An extremely fortuitous card, one that foretold success in business and pretty much anything else she put her mind to.

Victoria appeared to relax when I explained the card's meaning, although I could tell she didn't know much about Tarot and might not have been fazed if I turned up the Tower card, or the Devil. "Well, that's good to hear," she said, her big blue eyes lively with interest. "What's next?"

"Let's see," I replied, and pulled the next card.

The World. Another card that signified good luck, plans come to fruition, all the things people wanted to see when they had a reading. I relayed that information to Victoria, who gave a disbelieving shake of her head.

"This is all sounding too good to be true," she

remarked, and I gave a philosophical lift of my shoulders.

"Sometimes it's hard to accept the good things that come into our life," I said. "Just relax and know the future is looking bright."

And as I spoke, I pulled the third and final card of the spread.

The Lovers.

At once, her brows lifted. "Does this mean my love life will be looking up, too?" she asked, a note of laughter back in her voice.

"It might," I said. "The Lovers card is sometimes all about harmony, and not particularly romantic love. In this context, it's hard for me to say."

Despite my best efforts, I couldn't quite prevent myself from shooting a glance in Archie's direction. He was pretending to be asleep, but from the way his ears were tilted forward, I knew he was absorbing every single word.

Was he hoping the Lovers card might be referring to him?

A vain hope, considering he was still a cat. But....

"Well," Victoria said. "That was a pretty good reading. And I have to admit I'm ready to get back out there. I guess we'll just have to see."

I nodded, figuring I'd better leave it there.

"And it's past eight," she went on. "I need to

get back and check my email, and I should probably give you a little quiet time. But thanks very much for inviting me over."

"Oh, you're welcome," I said. "Let me show you where I keep Archie's food, and then I'll get you those spare keys to the place."

After a quick detour to point out the shelf in the pantry where the cat food resided, I went back to the office and got my spare set of keys out of the top desk drawer. When I returned, I found Victoria bending down and petting Archie, who'd apparently decided to stop pretending to be asleep so he could get in some last-minute caresses.

"Here you go," I said, and she straightened so she could take the keys from me. "I really appreciate you coming by to take care of him."

"I'm glad to do it," she replied. "He really is a gorgeous cat. And so friendly!"

Somehow, I managed to avoid exploding with laughter at that comment, and murmured something in agreement before I saw her to the door and we said our goodbyes. Afterward, I shut the door and glared down at the cat.

"That was a bit much, don't you think?"

"No," he said, sounding wounded. "She's a very friendly person, and so I responded in kind. I don't see anything wrong with that, do you?"

About fifty different answers sprang to my

lips, but I dismissed them all. I only said, "You'd better be on your best behavior tomorrow."

"When am I not?" he returned, and stalked out of the room.

Since it really wasn't worth getting into it with him, I went into the kitchen to rinse off the dinner plates and put them in the dishwasher. As I worked, though, something kept nagging at me.

That card pull I'd just done for Victoria had felt oddly familiar, as if I'd seen it somewhere before.

I closed the dishwasher, and then it hit me.

Back in L.A., I'd pulled almost those same cards for myself when deciding whether or not to leave town before Lucien Dumond caught up with me. True, I'd pulled the Tower first, indicating massive change was on the way, but I'd also drawn the World, and then the Ace of Pentacles and finally the Lovers.

My gaze strayed toward the hallway where Archie had disappeared. Was fate about to step in for Victoria and my cursed cat in a very big way?

This could all be coincidence, of course, and yet....

Well, I supposed we'd all find out either way soon enough.

11

Drinking Gilbert Grapes

My mother texted me a little past nine-thirty, letting me know they'd finally made it to the house safely.

Everything okay? I asked, feeling a bit trepidatious. I really should have gone out to the house to check on things that afternoon but had decided against it, mostly because I didn't want Susanna getting stirred up right before my family was due to arrive.

Yes, she replied. *Luisa did a great job. We're getting settled now. See you tomorrow!*

See you then! I replied, relieved beyond measure that it didn't sound as though the ghost had gotten up to any mischief in my absence. Maybe she really had been scared straight.

Whatever the reason for the continuing quiet at the Bigelow mansion, it meant I could sleep well that night—after exchanging texts with Calvin—and not worry about facing some catastrophe when I showed up at the mansion the next day. Our appointment at the spa in Gilbert was at one-thirty, which meant we needed to leave a little after noon. Not the most convenient timing, but I'd told my mother I'd get sandwiches and drinks for everyone from Cloud Coffee, and we could eat our lunch in the limo on the way out of town.

Yes, a limo. I'd protested the expense—especially since it had to come all the way out to Globe from Tempe to pick us up, only to turn around and head back to the greater Phoenix metro area—but my mother had insisted.

"It would be silly for all of us to be driving in different cars," she'd pointed out, and I'd decided it wasn't worth the argument.

So, after I'd collected everyone's orders and picked up the food, I headed out to the mansion to meet everyone. When I pulled up, the limo wasn't there yet, although I spotted Tom's Porsche Cayenne and an Audi SUV I didn't recognize, probably Tony and Madison's. On the other side was a Lexus sedan that I thought belonged to Nick, Tom's son. They were all parked off to one side of the garage, most likely to keep the driveway open for the limo, and also to ensure that the garage wouldn't be blocked when it came time to extract all the tables and chairs.

I went up the front steps and knocked, and at once my mother opened the door and enveloped me in a hug—well, after rescuing the tray of iced teas and bag of sandwiches, and placing them on a nearby side table.

"Oh, Selena," she said. "I can't believe your big day is almost here!"

To be honest, I couldn't quite believe it, either. All these months and all this planning, and we only had two days to go. "I know," I replied with a smile. At the same time, though, I couldn't help but shoot a furtive glance around, looking for any signs of supernatural activity. Yes, my mother hadn't mentioned anything like that, and yet I figured it couldn't hurt to be safe. At any rate, I didn't see anything that raised any alarms, and so it looked as though Susanna was still behaving herself.

"By the way," my mother went on, her brow now furrowing slightly. "What on earth is that jar filled with crystals and cinnamon sticks and bits of bark sitting on the desk in the upstairs office?"

Obviously, she'd found the spell jar. I supposed I should have known she'd notice it, since in general, anything that was even a hint out of place would catch her eye. Never mind that there wasn't any reason for her to have gone in there; she'd probably done a sweep of the whole house when they got in the night before, just to reassure herself it really had been cleaned properly and everything was up to her exacting standards.

"Um, it's a spell jar," I said, then added quickly as her frown deepened, "Just something for good luck. That's all."

Honestly, that was just a teeny little lie. On the other hand, one could say that being magically protected promoted good luck, so I wasn't completely mischaracterizing the thing.

"Oh," she said, expression brightening. "That was nice of you."

"It's nothing," I replied as I did my best not to flush.

But then Madison came down the stairs, and I managed to plaster a smile on my mouth. I knew it was absolutely none of my business what she did with her father's money, but it still annoyed me to think that Tom had probably paid for her Botox and her highlights, and most likely the chest that stretched the tight pink T-shirt she wore. Her husband Tony ostensibly worked for a financial planning firm, although I'd thought on more than one occasion that he must not be very good at his job, considering the way they were always "borrowing" money from Tom.

"Hi, Selena," Madison said, and stepped off the bottom stair so she could give me a hug, one that felt a lot less genuine than the embrace I'd gotten from my mother a few minutes earlier. "Are you excited?"

"Definitely," I said. "How was the drive?"

"Oh, fine," she replied, although the pursing of her lips that accompanied her answer told me she'd been annoyed by the road trip and would much rather have flown. However, since her father was paying for the whole outing, she'd had to go along with the plans Tom and my mother had made, even if she didn't like them very much.

Then Staci, Nick's wife, came down the stairs as well, and I had to repeat the ritual hug and accept her false congratulations. Or maybe they were real; with that side of the family, it was sometimes hard to tell.

At any rate, I was saved from any further excruciating chitchat by another knock at the door, one that turned out to be from Hazel. She came in and I made the introductions, glad that my best friend was so natural and uncontrived— and so much prettier—when contrasted with Tom's daughter and daughter-in-law.

I could tell they weren't too impressed, judging by the side-eye they gave one another after noting Hazel's faded Levi's and her definitely non-designer sleeveless top. But it was a warm shade of sage that lit up her green-hued eyes, and she certainly looked presentable, if not quite ready to go shopping on Rodeo Drive.

Which was fine, since that wasn't where we were headed. Speaking of which, the limo driver knocked on the door right after that, and then there was a mad dash to get all of us and our lunches inside the stretched SUV and on our way.

Hazel sat on one side of me and my mother on the other, a placement no one could really argue with, considering Hazel was my maid-of-honor. Once we were all settled, though, and the limo driver had begun to navigate his way down the winding road that led to Highway 60, Madison sent me a concerned glance I didn't believe for a moment and said, "I thought you were going to have four bridesmaids, Selena."

"I am," I said calmly after I finished sipping some iced green tea through the straw of my drink. "But Terry Woodrow—she's my friend Josie's niece-in-law—couldn't get off work today. She'll be at the rehearsal dinner tomorrow night, though."

"Oh, that's too bad," Madison replied, although, since she sent a quick glance at her sister-in-law, who smirked in return, I guessed she wasn't too sorry about the situation. No, she was probably pitying the poor working stiff who couldn't even get a day off to go have fun.

I didn't bother to correct that impression.

Terry had told me right from the start that, although she'd love to be one of my attendants, she wouldn't be able to take any days off work because she was hoarding her vacation time for a planned trip to Hawaii with the family. And of course, I'd told her she didn't need to worry about it, and having her there on the day of the wedding would be more than enough. Madison could think whatever she wanted.

Luckily, though, the conversation after that turned toward our spa afternoon, with Madison and Staci asking about Gilbert, and both Hazel and I assuring them that its downtown area was lots of fun and very cute. No, it wasn't Beverly Hills, but I thought they should be pretty happy with its offerings nonetheless.

When we got there, I could tell that the spa, with its desert-inspired décor and sleek granite floors and counters, impressed them somewhat, or at least, they were reassured that I hadn't taken them to some kind of strip-mall nail salon straight out of *Better Call Saul.* Massages first, with Hazel and my mother and me in one room, and Madison and Staci in another. I hadn't really planned it that way, but somehow my mother managed to maneuver the spa attendants so we were safely segregated from Tom's side of the family.

"You are a saint," I told my mom as the

masseuse started to knead my shoulders. Ah, that felt good. It wasn't until right then that I realized how much tension I'd been carrying in my upper body.

My mother chuckled, although the sound was a little muffled, thanks to the way she had her face down on the massage table and sticking through the little cut-out to accommodate her. "I guess I'm just used to them. Luckily, since they all live over on the Westside, our paths don't cross all that much except for on birthdays and holidays, that kind of thing." She paused there, and even though I couldn't see her expression, I got the feeling she'd frowned a little. "Although I have to say I wish they'd stop pestering Tom to sell the Encino house and move out to Pacific Palisades."

"Do you really think he'd do that?" I asked, trying not to wince as the masseuse began working on an especially tight knot between my shoulder blades. This whole ghostly mess must have made me even tenser than I'd thought.

"No," my mother replied, and I let myself relax a little on her behalf. "Tom loves that house, and he wants to be close to his business. He still doesn't have any intention of retiring, mostly because he knows he'd have to sell the company rather than try leaving it to his kids. They'd run it into the ground in a year."

On my other side, Hazel made an amused

noise that sounded almost like a snort. She'd heard stories from me, but now that she'd met Madison and Nick in person, she'd been able to take their measure for herself…and they'd definitely come up wanting.

It was a little sad, though, that Tom felt he had to keep working because his kids couldn't be trusted with the family business. Selling plumbing supplies weren't exactly glamorous, but judging by his and my mother's lifestyle—and the lifestyle he'd been able to provide for his children—they definitely paid the rent…and a whole lot more.

"But that's fine," my mother went on, her tone turning brisk. "Honestly, I don't know what Tom would do with himself if he stopped working. And actually, he has cut back on his hours, has time to golf most days, for us to go on vacation whenever we like, so I can't really complain."

No, she couldn't. My mother had worked hard all her life to make sure the two of us always had a decent place to live and that I went to good schools, so it made me happy to see her finally in a position where she could relax and have some fun.

It seemed she'd had enough of that topic, though, because she said next, "And what about you, Selena?"

"What about me?" I returned, not sure what she was driving at. "You're not expecting me to stop working after I marry Calvin, are you? That's a little too 1950s for me."

That comment earned me a chuckle. "No, of course not," my mother said, then paused so she could turn over, one hand keeping her protective towel firmly in place. "But you're also not going to need your apartment after you move in with him. What are you going to do with it? Rent it out?"

I'd already wrestled with that question a good bit and still hadn't come up with a decent solution. It was probably an irrational reaction, but some part of me didn't like the thought of someone I didn't know living there. At the same time, though, it seemed silly to let the place just stand there empty.

"Maybe," I said. "I really haven't figured it out yet. I guess after Calvin and I get back from our honeymoon, we'll sit down and talk it over."

This answer seemed to be good enough for my mother, because she nodded and then closed her eyes, clearly content at that point to just relax and let the masseuse do her work.

Probably a good idea. The whole point of this day was to indulge ourselves and get some heavy-duty relaxation in before the final push to make sure everything was ready for the wedding. My apartment wasn't going anywhere, so I could worry about that later.

Even as I closed my own eyes and did my best

to set all my worries aside, I didn't know how successful I was being. My thoughts couldn't seem to stop fretting about the ghost, about what I could do to ensure she wouldn't cause any more trouble before the wedding…or, even worse, during it. What if I actually had to halt the ceremony so Father Estevez could come in and handle my pesky spirit? That kind of incident would provide Globe with gossip fodder to last for months, if not years, not to mention ruining my special moment with Calvin.

Well, there was nothing I could do about it right now.

And actually, as the afternoon moved on to our mani/pedi sessions, and then to wine tasting at Garage East, Calvin's and my favorite place to get away for a special drink in Gilbert, I did find myself relaxing a bit. The change of scenery probably had something to do with it, and even Madison and Stacy became a lot more tolerable after they got some wine in them. By the time we finally piled in the SUV limo at a little after seven-thirty, following an indulgent meal at the same New Orleans–themed restaurant that Calvin and I tended to visit whenever we came to town, I was feeling pretty mellow.

Of course, that mellow sensation lasted roughly as long as it took to climb the walk to the Bigelow mansion, where all the lights blazed forth from the ground-floor rooms. I'd noticed that Tom's car was back in its spot by the garage, and so the guys must have returned from their golf expedition.

When we walked into the house, it was to find Calvin, Tom, Nick, and Tony standing there in the foyer, staring blankly at the mess confronting them. For a second or two, my brain didn't want to take in the jumble of clothes, shoes, underwear, and toiletries...until I realized what the disaster zone actually represented.

It looked exactly like someone had taken all of our visitors' belongings and thrown them down the stairs.

And it didn't take me too long to realize who had to be responsible.

Calvin looked more resigned than anything, while the other three men wore expressions ranging from confusion to outrage. "Looks like your resident ghost is at it again," my fiancé remarked.

"'Ghost'?" Madison demanded. She'd already brushed past me and was staring down at the mess scattered across the shining wooden floor. "What ghost?"

"Oh, the mansion's haunted," I said, hoping my blithe tone might stave off the coming explosion...and realizing that was probably unrealistic of me.

"'Haunted'?" Madison all but screeched, while Staci took a step back, as though putting some distance between herself and the scatter of clothes on the floor might somehow protect her from any further ghostly depredations.

My mother didn't quite roll her eyes, but I could tell she wasn't too thrilled by her daughter-in-law's assault on her eardrums. "Well, *supposedly* the house is haunted," she said. "But there's never been any trouble before this."

"Right," I said. "Honestly, I think the ghost is just upset by all the commotion with the wedding. She's really pretty harmless."

Madison's face had turned splotchy red beneath its spray tan. "I don't call tossing my Prada shoes on the floor 'harmless'!"

Since I knew she couldn't be reasoned with, I only said, "Calvin and I will help you pick up. And then I'll try to have a little chat with our ghost."

No one looked especially pleased by this offer; I could tell my mother and Tom were probably thinking that his kids and their spouses could pick up their own clothes, while I had to imagine Madison was weighing the pros and cons of bailing out then and there and checking in to the local Best Western, which was the only decent hotel in town.

However, since I knew Madison wouldn't be

caught dead in a Best Western, I had a feeling she'd rather put up with the ghost rather than risk news of her staying in a two-star hotel somehow reaching the ears of her Pacific Palisades friends. Grumbling under her breath, she started gathering up her things, and everyone else followed suit with their own belongings.

I took a step forward, and my mother said, "I think we have it all handled here, Selena. Why don't you go talk to your ghost and see if you can get this straightened out?"

Easier said than done, but on the other hand, trying to cajole Susanna into good behavior still seemed more appealing than picking up my in-laws' unmentionables. Calvin gamely pitched in, although I could tell he was doing his best to only gather the guys' stuff.

Probably a good idea.

I made my way up the stairs to the front office. Someone had already turned on all the lights, so at least I didn't have to worry about blundering around in the dark.

The spell jar still sat on the desk. Fat lot of good it had done.

"Susanna Caroline Bigelow!" I called out. The irritated snap to my voice sounded exactly like my mother's had back in the day when I was a kid and she was calling me to account for something or other. In a way, I wanted to chuckle; I wondered if I'd sound the same when I was ready to give Calvin's and my kids what-for.

But that day was still off in the future somewhere, so I needed to attend to the problem at hand.

My pesky poltergeist didn't seem too eager to make an appearance, since I still couldn't see hide nor hair of her.

"Susanna!" I snapped.

Very gradually, she materialized a few feet from where I stood. There was something almost insolent about the slow roll of her appearance, since other times she'd popped in and out of existence in pretty much the blink of an eye.

"What?" she asked, trying to look innocent, but a corner of her mouth was quirking and I knew she was trying to hold back a grin.

"Throwing people's clothes all over the floor is completely unacceptable," I said. "After spending a hundred years in this house, you can live with visitors for a couple of days."

Mentioning the length of her tenure in the house apparently had been a misstep, though, because her brows drew together and she retorted, "I don't want them here!"

"Well, we all have to deal with a lot of things in life we don't want to," I said calmly. "But I'm warning you again—I've got Father Estevez on speed dial, and I'd be all too happy to give him a call and have him up here to perform an exorcism."

Did a ghost from 1921 even know what speed dial was? Of course, it was a relic of the past, just like Susanna herself, but I'd always kind of liked the expression.

One way or another, my threat seemed to have sunk in. A ghost couldn't exactly go pale, but Susanna was definitely looking a little pinched.

"You wouldn't!"

"Oh, yes, I would," I returned. "I don't want to, but if there's one more disruption inside this house, I'm getting him up here immediately."

For a second or two, the ghost was silent. Then a little smile I didn't like very much touched the corners of her mouth, and she said, "Very well. No more disruptions here."

And she promptly disappeared.

Footsteps on the landing outside made me turn. A disgruntled group of houseguests was trooping past the office, laden with the contents of their luggage. Or at least, Tom's kids looked angry; he and my mother appeared tired more than anything else, and I couldn't blame them for that. Having to stop and collect all their belongings at the end of a long day certainly couldn't have been any fun.

Calvin brought up the rear. He had an armful

of shoes, and lifted an eyebrow at me as he passed, although he didn't say anything.

"It's okay," I called out as I stepped into the doorway. "She's gone. And she won't be bothering you again."

"Did you get it in writing?" Nick quipped, although I got the impression the question was only half-joking.

"Let's just say I made the ghost aware of the consequences of messing with your stuff," I replied. "So I'm pretty sure everything is going to be fine from here on out." My gaze moved toward my mother and Tom as I added, "But just call me if it isn't."

"We'll be fine," she said crisply. The no-nonsense expression she wore told me she wouldn't call and disrupt my sleep this close to the wedding even if the ghost decided to drop all their beds out on the front lawn. "You go on home, Selena. We'll see you tomorrow."

Right. Friday was the all-important day when the pavilions would be delivered and set up, along with the seating for the lounge areas. Because the people at Panorama Party Rentals had been such an enormous pain in the behind, Victoria had hired some local movers to come out Saturday morning and put out the chairs for the ceremony, as well as moving all the dining tables into the main pavilion. They'd be on standby to relocate the chairs for the ceremony when the time came, since way back when we were booking everything, Josie and I had decided to save money by reusing the chairs rather than renting two sets.

Just as well, I thought darkly. *We would never have been able to fit that many chairs in the garage.*

Calvin and I said goodbye to the group, and then we both headed down the stairs and let ourselves out. The night air was mild and scented with roses and freshly mown grass, and I really wished the two of us could just go back to his place and sit out under the moon and sip some wine.

But I needed to get home to Archie, and Calvin and I had already agreed to spend these last few days leading up to the wedding at our respective homes as sort of a way of saying goodbye to our past lives before moving on to our shared existence.

He walked me to my car, though, and we shared a few kisses under a pretty little crescent moon that hung low in the west. After we pulled apart, he glanced up at the mansion, looking innocent enough with all its windows aglow.

"Do you really think she's going to behave herself?"

"She'd better," I said. "I threatened to sic Father Estevez on her, and that seemed to have done the trick. Of course, I tried that threat before and didn't get very far, but I think this time she could tell I'd lost my patience."

"Let's hope so." Calvin reached over and squeezed my hand. "It's going to be okay. We're in the home stretch now."

It didn't feel that way. I felt as though I was barely halfway through a marathon. But he was right—we only had to get through Friday and part of the day Saturday, and then the wedding would be a done deal, and we could relax and drink champagne at the reception.

Lots and lots of champagne.

"I know." I went on my tiptoes and kissed him on the cheek. "Thank you for going golfing with the guys today."

He grinned, teeth flashing in the light from the security lamps mounted under the garage eaves. "Oh, it wasn't so bad. Nick cheats, though."

"Why does that not surprise me?"

I got a chuckle in response to that rhetorical question, and then Calvin opened my car door so I could get in. "What time do you want me over here tomorrow?" he asked.

"Around ten-thirty, maybe? I'm sure Victoria is going to have it all handled, but I still want to be on-site to make sure everything gets set up in the right place."

"Will do. And then I'm taking you out to lunch afterward."

Good thing I hadn't gone for a super form-fitting dress, or all these big meals might have spelled disaster. Luckily, I refused to be one of those brides who starved herself for weeks before the ceremony, so I knew I'd be fine.

"It's a date."

Another kiss, this one with him leaning down as I sat in the driver's seat, and then he shut the door and began walking over to the spot where he'd parked his official-issue Durango.

Time to head home. Tomorrow was going to be another long day.

12

Transformations

ALL SEEMED QUIET WHEN I GOT HOME AT A little past nine. Victoria had thoughtfully left on one of the lamps in the living room when she'd come in to feed Archie, as well as the under-cabinet lights in the kitchen, and so I didn't have to walk into a dark apartment.

"Archie?" I called out, since I didn't see any sign of him when I looked around. True, at that time of night, he probably had retired to his bed in the office, but still, it wasn't like him not to greet me with some sort of snarky comment about taking my sweet time to come home.

To my surprise, he crawled out from under-neath the coffee table a moment later, his gaze not meeting mine.

"Is everything all right?" I asked next, since

this behavior was very unlike him. Had he had an accident somewhere?

No, that didn't make much sense. My cursed cat was fastidious in the extreme; he'd never once misbehaved in all the time he'd been living with me.

His tail flicked back and forth, and he sat down on his haunches and sent me a poisonous glare. "No, everything is most definitely not all right."

Oh, boy. That tense scene at the Bigelow mansion had pretty much undone all the masseuse's work from early that day, and I could practically feel my shoulders tighten at the anger in Archie's voice.

"Did something happen with Victoria?" I ventured.

For a moment, Archie didn't reply. His tail kept making those irritated twitches, and so I knew something was up. At last he said, "I thought I could do it. I thought it would be enough just to spend some time with her, but it wasn't. And you know why?"

Of course I did, but I really didn't want to get into that right now. The only thing I wanted was to face-plant on my pillow and stay in bed for roughly ten hours.

However, it didn't look as though that was going to happen, and so I let out a breath and said, "Because she didn't stay long enough? I know she still had a lot of work to do, and—"

"No, that's not it," he said brusquely, cutting me off mid-sentence. "Or at least, that was part of it, but not all. No, it's because I'm still a damn cat!"

Since my eyes were functioning just fine, I knew that as well as he did. Still, we'd come to almost the day of the wedding, and I had to admit that the chances of my finding a way to turn him back into a man at this point were roughly the same as getting chosen for NASA's astronaut program.

"I'm sorry, Archie," I said. "I really did try everything I could. I'm just not that kind of a witch. I can't turn people into frogs, or cats, or whatever, and I certainly have no idea how to undo that sort of spell."

And I was truly sorry. I'd lost count of how much money I'd spent on spell books that didn't work and ingredients for potions that ended up getting poured down the drain, but it wasn't the money that mattered. I would have happily spent a million dollars getting Archie returned to his true form if I'd thought it would work. Despite his sometimes annoying nature, he was sort of like the brother I'd never had, someone I felt responsible for.

But none of those spells and potions had worked. None of them.

Something must have shifted in my expression, because some of the angry glitter left Archie's golden eyes, and his furry little head drooped.

"I know," he said, gaze fixed on the living room rug, which bore the scars of numerous scratch-fests. "I know you did your best. And before I met Victoria, I might have been—well, not resigned, precisely, but more able to live with the situation. Now, though…."

The words trailed off there, but I thought I understood what he was trying to say. His previous seventy years of existence as a cat might not have been the most rewarding thing in the world, and yet he'd managed to keep going, to take each day at a time because he didn't think anything about his future would ever change. After Victoria entered his life, and he came to the startling realization that it wasn't that he had no interest in romance at all, but only had to meet the right person to desire such a thing, his furry little body must have felt like a prison.

"She'll be gone soon," I said softly. "I know it's hard, but at least when she's done with the wedding, she'll move on. And I'll be here with you through all of it."

"Will you, though?" Archie retorted. "You're heading off to California on Sunday and leaving me with Hazel. I wouldn't exactly call that being there for me. I love Victoria, and there's absolutely nothing you can do to help me."

The second those words left his mouth, an odd shimmer started to swirl around him. I stared, wide-eyed, as his cat body began to stretch and shift, to become bigger and bigger, to start turning into…

…well, to start turning into a man.

My wide-eyed shock lasted for about a second, and then I hurried over to the couch and grabbed the afghan I had draped over the back. I tossed it toward Archie, who reached out with an oddly human arm and wrapped it around himself.

Because of that makeshift shield, I didn't get to see the rest of the transformation. Less than a minute passed, though, and then there he was, standing on two legs that didn't seem entirely steady, the afghan he had clutched around him not completely concealing a chest and shoulders and arms that appeared more muscular than I might have imagined.

He blinked. As I'd thought upon seeing his photo in an old yearbook, his true eye color was a shade somewhere between blue and gray, although slightly more on the gray side. And he was a lot taller than I'd expected—not as tall as Calvin, but still several inches above six feet. Probably around the same age, too, in his mid-thirties, showing how Archie really hadn't aged a day since that fateful moment when a witch had decided to teach him a lesson and turn him into a cat.

Our eyes met, and I smiled. Once again, the universe had shown me that I needed to trust it.

"Welcome back, Archie," I said.

Shock registered on every inch of his finely sculpted screen-idol features. And his voice sounded just the same as it always had…not quite tenor, not quite baritone, but somewhere in the middle. "What—what happened?"

This was probably the first time I'd ever seen Archie Bradshaw at a loss. Then again, considering the circumstances, I thought I could understand why he looked so gobsmacked. The Goddess only knew that I felt as if the universe was spinning around me, so the sensation must have been a hundred times worse for my former feline.

He needed me to be here for him, though, and so I did my best to pull myself together.

"I have a theory," I said with a smile. "But maybe you'd like to change into your new clothes first?"

Another blink, before he looked down at his afghan-wrapped body and ventured, "And have a shower?"

Good thing I kept the guest bathroom stocked, even though I never had houseguests. But my mother had taught me to be prepared for any situation…although I doubted she could have ever imagined a situation like this.

"Absolutely," I said, then added, "There's also a little packet with an unused travel toothbrush and some toothpaste in one of the bathroom drawers."

Looking relieved, Archie clutched the afghan around him even tighter and hurried from the room. A few minutes later, the water in the hallway bathroom came on.

I realized my hands still shook. Pouring a glass of wine that late in the evening probably wasn't a very good idea, and so I instead headed into the kitchen and put on the kettle. If I were any judge, I'd hazard a guess that Archie could also use a cup of tea when he emerged from the shower.

That was why I set out a teapot and two cups on the coffee table, along with some butter cookies I'd made a few days earlier. Maybe not the biggest feast to welcome Archie back to human life, but it was a start.

He seemed to take a long time in the bathroom. That was all right; he was catching up on missing years of hot showers. When he did appear, he looked a little less freaked out, although maybe that was the clothes. He'd put on a button-up blue shirt and crisp khaki slacks, and looked more like someone who'd wandered out of the pages of a Ralph Lauren catalog than a man who'd been trapped in a cat's body for the past seventy years.

"Tea?" I asked, and he smiled...actually smiled, showing a hint of a dimple in one cheek and some extremely straight white teeth.

I had a feeling Victoria Parrish wasn't going to know what hit her.

"Tea would be wonderful. Thank you."

He sat down in the armchair to one side of the couch and waited while I poured him a cup of Darjeeling. I had a feeling he might be an Earl Grey kind of guy, but since I didn't much care for that variety of tea, I didn't keep it on hand.

After he'd dropped one cube of sugar and a single spoonful of milk in his cup, he looked up at me. "You said you had a theory about all this?"

"Yes," I replied. "I mean, it's just a theory. I don't know for sure that it's true or not. But I think the curse that witch put on you all those years ago had the means of breaking it contained inside you all the time. She was angry with you that you wouldn't return her affections, and so she made the condition of breaking the curse that you had to fall in love with someone. She probably thought such a thing would never happen, and so she felt safe putting that little back door in there."

For a moment, Archie was silent, hands curved around the cup he held. It was a sturdy stoneware mug and not some fragile porcelain thing, but it still looked small with his strong, long-fingered hands engulfing it. I had to force myself not to stare, to not take in every single detail of his appearance, from the thick brown lashes that framed his blue eyes to the strong lines of his jaw. Yes, I'd seen that photo of him in a long-ago Globe High yearbook, and yet that wasn't the same thing as being physically in his presence.

He was just so darn *real.*

"I suppose I can see that," he said at length. "That is, there was some gossip in Globe about why I didn't seem interested in forming a relationship with any of the eligible women here in town. I tried to brush it off, of course, and even did my best to circulate the rumor that I'd had my heart broken by a woman back in Chicago and that was why I'd resettled here, but I don't think most people believed it. So it's entirely plausible the witch thought she'd cast an unbreakable spell on me."

"Joke's on her," I said lightly. Even as I spoke, though, the sheer enormity of what had just happened finally dawned on me. Archie was back…but he was a man without an identity. The man he'd been had been presumed dead years earlier. He didn't have a driver's license, a credit history, a place to stay.

Well, I could fix that last part at least. The rest we'd just have to figure out.

"I'm sorry there isn't a bed in the office," I told him. "But you can crash on the sofa here."

He glanced over at the couch where I sat and shook his head. "I wouldn't feel right cohabiting with a woman who's about to be married the day after tomorrow."

I wanted to laugh, but I knew he was being serious. "It's okay, Archie," I told him. "I don't think we're going to get up to any hanky-panky."

His mouth tightened. "Of course not," he retorted. "But it still doesn't feel right to me."

Great. I supposed I could send him to the Best Western, and yet I didn't really like that idea.

Then it came to me.

"Do you want to stay at Hazel's Airbnb?" I asked. I knew it was available, because she'd groused to me while we were getting our mani-pedis about how the people who'd rented it for the weekend had canceled it at the last minute, leaving her high and dry. "It's not too far away, but at least you'd have your own space until we can get things figured out."

Immediately, his expression brightened. "I think that sounds like a very good idea."

And so I got on the phone, apologizing to Hazel for calling her so late, but letting her know that my cousin Archie had been able to make it to Globe for the wedding after all, and so would she be okay if he stayed in her vacation rental for a few days?

"'Archie'?" Hazel echoed, sounding puzzled. "You named your cat after your cousin?"

"Um, yes," I said as I did my best to think quickly and manufacture a story that would sound halfway plausible. "We used to play together when we were kids, so I guess that's what popped into my head when I was trying to come up with a name for the cat."

"Okay." For a second, I feared she was going to ask some more probing questions, since I'd never mentioned anything about cousins to her before this…mostly because, as the only child of an only child, I really didn't have any. To my relief, however, she just went on, "The code for the front door lock is 2276. I had everything prepped for the people who canceled on me, so there are fresh sheets on the bed and fresh towels in the bathroom, and there's coffee and stuff in the pantry. Not a lot of food, though, but there are some oatmeal packets if your cousin gets hungry."

"We'll figure something out," I replied. "Thanks so much, Hazel—I really appreciate it."

"No worries," she said. "See you tomorrow night at the rehearsal dinner!"

"Absolutely."

We ended the call, and I looked over to see

Archie watching me intently. "All settled," I said. "Let's get your stuff packed up—you can borrow one of my suitcases for now. I just need it back before the wedding."

"So you can pack for your honeymoon," he observed, but he definitely didn't look as bent out of shape at the prospect as he might have been when he was a cat. I got the feeling he was already thinking of all the freedom he would have now that he was a man again.

Including not getting shipped off to stay with Hazel during the time Calvin and I were out of town. I'd need to work out something with her longer-term, maybe see if she'd give our newly human Archie a monthly rate, but for now, the most important thing was that he had a place to land and didn't have to worry about sleeping on my couch.

The suitcase was stored in the office closet as well, so I sent Archie off to pack his clothes. When he came back out, rolling the suitcase behind him, I said, "You'll need some odds and ends besides the clothes. Good thing the Super Walmart is open until eleven."

He cocked an eyebrow at me. Funny how his facial expressions seemed oddly familiar, even though they were being translated through human features rather than feline ones. "'Odds and ends'?"

"Well, a full-size toothbrush and toothpaste… deodorant…shampoo, that kind of thing. Oh, and a phone."

For a second, his mouth opened, as if he wanted to argue with me, but he closed it again just as quickly. Most likely, he was thinking of how much time people in the twenty-first century spent on their cellphones, and how of course he would need one to fit in.

We went downstairs to my car. After Archie had loaded his suitcase in the luggage compartment, I headed out to the highway. He looked at the digital instrumentation on the dashboard with some interest, and I asked, "Do you know how to drive?"

He immediately drew himself up. "Of course I know how to drive," he retorted with some indignation. A moment of silence as he glanced at the dashboard again, and then he added in a much more subdued tone, "Although I may need a refresher."

"Well, we probably won't have time for that before the wedding," I said. "I'll see if I can get Travis Cox—he's Globe's only Uber driver—to get you around in the interim. We can make up some story about your driver's license getting stolen— that'll also answer any other questions about why you don't have a current I.D."

This comment seemed to subdue Archie,

because his brows pulled together as he considered all the little bits and pieces he'd need to resume his life some seventy years after it had taken an abrupt left turn.

First things first, though.

We pulled into the parking lot of the Super Walmart, which seemed surprisingly crowded for nine-thirty at night. But then, I supposed someone might need to stop in for a few things after getting off a shift at the Freeport mine, or maybe a lot of people had just gotten a hankering for chips and salsa during a Netflix binge.

Whatever the reason, the place was anything but a ghost town. Archie's eyes widened as we entered the store and he took his first look around.

"This is what a grocery store looks like now?"

"It's what a Super Walmart looks like," I said, doing my best to repress a smile. While Archie had done a lot of wandering around Globe during his seventy years as a cat, I still doubted he would have been able to waltz into the superstore and start exploring the place, and TV shows and commercials weren't any kind of a replacement for experiencing the real thing. "It's kind of a combination of a grocery store and a general retail store. Anyway, we should be able to get you a lot of what you need to get started."

I began rolling the cart toward the consumer

electronics section, figuring one of the first orders of business was to buy him a phone of some sort. Since he didn't have a license or a credit card, I had to settle for a cheapie little burner phone, the kind you could fill up by purchasing preloaded cards in various denominations. A couple hundred bucks would be enough to get him started, and hopefully by the time he ran through all that, we would have figured out how to get him an up-to-date driver's license and a bank account that could provide him with a Visa debit card.

So many things he needed—a wallet, and all sorts of personal sundries. I let him choose, which seemed to take an inordinate amount of time, since he seemed compelled to pick up each item and turn it over in his hands, read the label, and then decide whether or not it was going home with him.

Good thing the store was open until eleven.

Eventually, though, we made it to the grocery section. I noticed how he disdained the prepack-aged food, and instead got a canister of real oatmeal, bread, milk, bacon, and eggs, and a bunch of fresh produce.

"I've been craving a peach for at least sixty years," he said as he lifted a particularly plump specimen and held it to his nose, taking an appre-ciative sniff. Then he added it to the plastic bag he held, looking pleased with himself.

"'Do you dare to eat a peach?'" I quipped, and he lifted an eyebrow.

"Quoting T.S. Eliot, Ms. Marx?" he said. "You surprise me."

"Hey, I remember a few things from AP English," I returned, and he actually smiled.

"It's good to know the educational system in this country hasn't gone to complete wrack and ruin."

I'd heard other opinions to the contrary, but since I didn't have any recent firsthand experience, I only made a noncommittal sound. It seemed that Archie was more interested in the produce, anyway, because he moved on to add a package of cherries to the cart.

After that, though, it appeared he was satisfied, because he said, "That should be enough to get me started, I think."

One had to hope. He'd certainly piled on enough groceries to last him a week or more, depending on how much he ate at home and whether he would venture out to get something from a local restaurant.

Speaking of which—

I got a hundred dollars in cash when we checked out, the most they'd allow. As Archie and I were walking back to the car, I handed him the wad of twenties.

"Take this," I said. "I'll try to get you some

more tomorrow morning before I head over to the Bigelow house to oversee the setup, but it should be enough to get you started."

His mouth opened, as if he wanted to protest, but then he closed it again and silently stashed the money in his pants pocket. Most likely, he'd realized that he'd landed in the twenty-first century with pretty much nothing to his name, and so he couldn't let his pride get in the way of survival.

Once we were out of the parking lot and headed over to Hazel's Airbnb, however, he said, "Thank you for all this. I'll find some way to pay you back."

"That's not necessary," I replied at once. "I'm more than happy to do whatever it takes to get you set up in this time and place. You just need to do your best to roll with it."

His jaw tightened a bit, but he didn't argue, only gave a resigned nod. "Still…thank you."

Only two words…but important ones. And they were a lot coming from Archie, who definitely had never been the effusive type when he was a cat and didn't show much indication of changing his stripes now.

The rest of the car ride—such as it was—was spent in silence. I turned onto Hazel's street and then pulled up into the driveway. Her house had a small one-car garage tucked back from the street down a long driveway, but since she was currently using it for storage, I couldn't have parked there even if I wanted to.

Archie and I got out of the car and loaded up our plunder from Super Walmart. As we came around to the front porch, though, he stopped stock-still, eyes widening a bit.

"It's my house," he breathed.

"Well, it's a place to crash," I remarked.

He shook his head, expression filled with an odd sort of yearning, although for what, I didn't know.

"No, Selena," he said, his tone quiet but firm. "I'm saying it's *my* house. The one I was living in when that witch turned me into a cat."

Startled, I looked from him to the house and back again. Since the place had been built in the 1920s, of course it was entirely plausible that someone might have been living in it in the 1950s. Still, for it to be the exact same house....

Then I had to smile.

The universe had a way of setting things right, even if it might take a while. Who knew what convoluted path ownership of the house had taken in the years after Archie Bradshaw had mysteriously vanished? I had to believe he must have been declared dead at some point, and the house had either gone to someone he'd named as a beneficiary in his will, or, if not, had probably been sold at auction, setting up a chain of owner-ship that had ended with my friend Hazel.

"Well," I said lightly. "Let's see if you recognize the inside."

And I entered the code to unlock the door.

Archie looked around in some suspicion as I turned on the lights, but then he seemed to relax slightly. The house had been updated, of course, had new central air and a newish kitchen, and yet the bones of it remained intact; the mellow oak floors and the built-in bookcases on either side of the fireplace with its cheerful green tile surround were probably much the same as they had been back in his day.

Maybe that was just the slightest nod of approval. "The colors are a bit loud," he said. "But it looks like my house."

True, Hazel had painted the walls in cheerful colors, and the same friendly yellow/green/blue scheme continued throughout the house, but it wasn't as if the place had been decorated in shocking pink and bright orange. "I think it feels happy," I said. "Wait until you see it in daylight."

He might have shrugged. The most important thing, though, was to get his groceries in the refrigerator and the pantry, and then for him to head back out to the car so he could fetch his luggage and put away his clothes so he could return the borrowed suitcase to me. This procedure took some time, during which I sat on the couch and texted Calvin.

I've got some news about Archie.

Has something happened?

Yes, but in a good way, I wrote back. *Let's just say that Victoria's going to have to find a way to shoehorn in another guest at the reception.*

For a second, my phone remained mute. Then it pinged.

You mean...?

It seemed Calvin didn't want to put the notion into words, even in a text message.

Yes, I told him. *The curse is broken. I'm getting him settled in Hazel's Airbnb right now, since he needed a place to crash.*

That's amazing. How did you do it?

I didn't do anything. Archie managed it all on his own. But I'll explain when I see you tomorrow. I just wanted to give you a heads-up so you wouldn't get blindsided by the whole thing.

I could almost see the wry smile Calvin was probably wearing as he replied, *Thanks for that. Love you.*

Love you more.

He sent back a wink emoji, and that was the end of the exchange.

Archie came back into the living room just as I was about to put away my phone. "All settled?" I asked.

"I think so," he replied. "It still seems exceedingly odd that I'm going to be able to sleep in a bed like a real person, that I'm back in my house."

Although I could have pointed out that technically, it was Hazel's house, I didn't want to burst Archie's bubble like that. And who knew? Maybe I could convince her to sell it to me so I could gift it to him, but I figured that particular transaction could wait a while.

In the meantime, it was just good to know he'd be in a place where he felt safe.

"Can I have your phone?" I asked next. "We need to get it set up."

"Just a moment."

He came back with the little burner phone, still in its package. I popped it open, went through the setup procedure, and added fifty dollars' worth of minutes from one of the prepaid cards we'd bought. Soon enough, it was ready to go, so I went ahead and added both Calvin's and my phone numbers to the contacts list, and then Hazel's, just in case something came up with the house. Oh, and Travis's information, since Archie would need Globe's single solitary Uber driver to ferry him around while I was out of town.

And, after a brief pause, I put Victoria's phone number in there as well. Archie watched this operation, one eyebrow raised.

"Are you sure that's necessary?"

"Well," I said breezily, "you never know. It couldn't hurt…and it's not like you have to call her if you don't want to."

His expression turned almost hungry, and I guessed how much he wanted to do that very thing. However, he gave a shrug that didn't fool me for a minute and said, "I suppose we'll cross paths at the wedding. I can leave it there for now."

Right. Then again, a wedding was a very good place to meet a person…although I had something else in mind.

"Actually," I said, trying to sound casual and probably failing miserably, "would you come along with me to the Bigelow mansion tomorrow morning? You have such a good eye for things—it would really help to have your input as we're finalizing the setup."

Maybe Archie saw through this ploy and maybe he didn't, but I had to think that the appeal to his ego must have had some effect. "Of course," he replied. "What time?"

"I'll pick you up a little after ten."

"That should work."

With that settled, there didn't seem to be much else to do. While it felt anticlimactic to leave him alone after everything that had happened, I knew he needed some time to himself to adjust, to get used to his new reality.

And also, I was just bone-tired. It had turned out to be another horrendously long day.

I knew instinctively that Archie wasn't the huggy type, so instead I extended a hand to him after he walked me to the door. For a second, he stared down at it, then reached out and gave it a firm shake.

"Thank you again, Selena," he said quietly, but it was enough.

"Nothing to it," I replied. "Get a good night's sleep, and I'll see you in the morning."

After that, I made my way down the porch and got into my car. Archie remained silhouetted in the door for a moment, and then closed it slowly. A moment later, the porch lights went out.

I smiled. Yes, I was exhausted, but it was a good kind of tiredness. Something had just been set right in the world.

Now the only thing left was to figure out what to do about Susanna Bigelow.

13

In the Upside-Down

NOT GOING TO LIE—WHEN I WOKE UP THE next morning and walked into the kitchen, and realized I'd never have to fill Archie's bowls again, or make sure I had plenty of his favorite salmon treats stocked in the pantry, I got a little teary. Of course, I was happy for him, but at the same time, I'd gotten used to having him around. The apartment felt way too empty without him.

And as to how I was supposed to explain the disappearance of my cat, I wasn't quite sure. Then again, he'd been a street cat when he appeared on my balcony more than a year earlier, and I certainly let him roam outside whenever he wanted. If anyone asked, I could say that I'd let him out one day and he'd never come back.

A lie, sure…but there was no way in the world

I could tell anyone other than Calvin the real truth about Archie.

It will be fine, I told myself as I got some coffee going. After the day I'd had yesterday, I made sure to brew it extra strong. *You're going to be moving in with Calvin, and you won't be alone. And when you get back from your honeymoon, you can talk about getting a pet. Maybe a dog, since Archie was never exactly a cat. Not really.*

I had to admit that the idea of a dog appealed to me. The adorable little dogs at the Happy Tails Winery in Globe had shown me that small dogs didn't have to be yappy and annoying, and I'd never been able to have a dog because of spending all my life in rentals…until I moved here, anyway, and finally had my own place.

Just thinking about picking out a dog with Calvin cheered me a good bit, and some strong coffee and a bagel and eggs improved my mood that much more. And since I hadn't gotten any frantic texts or phone calls from my mother, I had to believe that Susanna had been quiescent the evening before.

Maybe she really had learned her lesson.

With that cheerful thought to buoy me, I went ahead and took a shower, then got dressed. Since we were going to be tromping around the Bigelow mansion's grounds for most of the morning, I dressed simply, in jeans and my favorite lime green Keds and a sleeveless white shirt with some pale green embroidery around the neckline.

Even getting ready, though, melancholy moved through me again, this time because I knew that after tomorrow, I wouldn't be putting on my makeup in front of this mirror again, or walking downstairs to open the shop. A new and exciting life beckoned, one I looked forward to with all my heart, but still, I'd have to say goodbye to the existence I'd created for myself here in Globe at the same time…and goodbyes were never easy.

Despite my seesawing emotions, I was out the door at ten and driving over to Archie's place—somehow, I'd already started thinking of the house that way—in such a bright, clear morning that it was impossible to feel too sad about anything. And after I'd pulled into the driveway and gone up the porch steps to knock on the front door, Archie answered right away, looking very natty in gray slacks and a white button-up shirt. Maybe a little overdressed for wandering the mansion's grounds, but since I couldn't really see him wearing jeans and a T-shirt, it would have to do.

"Right on time," he said, his tone almost approving.

"I do my best," I replied. "Sleep well?"

"Yes." He paused, and then added with a lift

at the corner of his mouth, "I must admit that there have been some technological advances over the last seventy years when it comes to mattresses."

Since I knew Hazel had outfitted the house with new memory foam beds when she decided to turn it into an Airbnb, I could see why Archie was impressed. "And in a few other areas as well," I said lightly. "But we should get going."

He came outside and entered the code for the door; it must have been written down in the guest packet Hazel had put together for her vacation renters. As we descended the porch stairs, however, he paused on the middle step so he could look around the neighborhood, at the bright flowers in the front yards and the variety of colors the houses had been painted...no such thing as an HOA in this part of town, that was for sure.

"It doesn't look as if it's changed very much," he observed. "The houses are different colors, of course, and the gardens are landscaped a little differently, but I would still recognize this neighborhood."

"I'm glad," I said. "It's always nice to have some continuity."

Archie nodded, and we went ahead and got in the car. Once again, he carefully watched everything I did while I drove, as if doing his best to familiarize himself with the layout of the instruments and to note the differences between this modern vehicle and the ones he'd driven back in the 1950s.

"I'll give you driving lessons when I get back," I promised. "Right now, though, I just want to get through the next forty-eight hours."

"You make it sound like an ordeal," he observed, the dry tone in his voice impossible to ignore.

"Oh, I'm looking forward to the wedding," I said quickly. The last thing I wanted was to give him the wrong impression. "But there's still a lot of prep involved, and I have no idea what kind of mischief Susanna is going to get up to between now and then."

"One can hope none at all," Archie responded. "However, I can understand your trepidation." He paused there, and sent me a sideways look from behind the Ray-Bans we'd mail-ordered months earlier. It didn't surprise me he'd chosen those sunglasses, since they were a little bit of something familiar in a very unfamiliar world. "And how are you going to explain me to your mother?" he went on. "You told Hazel I was your cousin, but of course your mother will know that's a lie."

"Cousin on my father's side," I said blithely. "She really doesn't know anyone from my father's family, and he's not coming to the wedding, so it's a great cover story."

Apparently, Archie didn't seem to think so. Expression almost aghast, he said, "Your father isn't coming to his own daughter's wedding?"

Even though Archie had gotten some of the bare bones of my life story, I hadn't told him everything. Shoulders lifting slightly, I replied, "He's never been a big part of my life. I mean, he paid child support, and he tried to see me on my birthdays and around the holidays when I was little, but we haven't had a lot of contact lately. It's fine—he's married and has his own family. I actually sent him an invitation to the wedding. He sent his regrets—it's his youngest daughter's birthday this weekend, and he couldn't get away. It's fine."

And it honestly was. Jordan Fairfield had never been anything close to a true father to me, so it wasn't as though I'd really regret him not being at the wedding. Tom had already agreed to walk me down the aisle, and that was just fine.

But because my biological father wouldn't be here, I'd be able to easily pass Archie off as a cousin on that side of the family. My mother might wonder why I'd invited a cousin I barely knew to my wedding, but if she asked, I'd just say that Archie and I had chatted on Facebook, and I wanted to have someone from the paternal side of things to attend the ceremony.

Maybe it was a bit of a stretch, but still not as awkward as trying to explain that Archie was actually the big gray cat who'd been living with me for the past year, newly turned back into a man.

We pulled up into the driveway but didn't get very far, since most of it was blocked by a couple of big trucks, obviously the rest of the party rental people here to drop off and set up the pavilions and the lounge seating areas. As best I could, I maneuvered the Beetle into the lee of the garage, making sure I left enough room for the trucks to back out when they were done unloading.

Just as Archie and I were getting out of the car, Calvin's big Durango came up the driveway as well. Seeing the lay of the land, he also made sure to park well out of the way, although, since his vehicle was so much bigger than mine, it still overhung the drive a bit.

He exited the vehicle, his gaze moving at once to my companion.

"Calvin," I said, walking quickly over to him with Archie only a foot or so behind, "this is my cousin, Archie Bradshaw."

Comprehension flared in Calvin's eyes. "Nice to meet you, Archie," he said, just the slightest wry inflection in those words telling me he knew exactly what was going on.

"And nice to meet you as well," Archie returned. "Or at least, to meet you in this form."

Calvin grinned, his white teeth flashing in the sunlight. "Yes, it sounds like you have a story to tell."

"It'll have to wait, though," I put in. "We need to get up to the house—it looks like the guys got here a little early."

Which was no more than the truth, because Victoria had told me they'd been slated to get here around ten-thirty and it was barely ten-fifteen. That probably explained why I hadn't seen her red Mercedes SUV parked with the rest of the vehicles.

The three of us made our way up the front path. A group of workmen were clustered on the porch, with one of them talking to my mother, who looked a little distracted. Relief was clear on her face as she turned toward my little trio, although I noticed the way her forehead puckered in puzzlement when her gaze fell on Archie.

"Good morning, Mom," I said, then turned to the party rental guys. "Hi, I'm Selena. We can go ahead and get set up."

"You're the bride?" the foreman asked. He was probably in his late thirties, with thinning blond hair pulled back into a ponytail and the ruddy complexion of someone whose skin really wasn't suited to searing desert sun.

"That's right," I said, and had to stop there, because Victoria had come hurrying up the walk. Since this was a work day, she was dressed a lot like me, in slim jeans and a simple shirt, although hers was pink and she had on flat sandals rather than tennis shoes.

At the sight of her, Archie went stock still, his gaze seeming to travel everywhere but her face. She barely seemed to notice him, instead saying to the man from the party-supply company, "I have all the layouts here," as she gestured with a clipboard she held. "Let me show you where we need everything set up."

And before Calvin or I could say anything, she'd led the guy down the porch and off toward the big lawn where the first pavilion would be erected.

Well, I suppose that's why we had a wedding planner. Still….

My mother sent a pointed look in Archie's direction, then glanced over at me. "Selena, are you going to introduce me to your friend?"

Here went nothing.

"Oh, right," I said. "Mom, this is Archie Bradshaw. He's one of my cousins on Jordan's side of the family."

She blinked. "I didn't know you were in touch with any of them."

"We sort of bumped into each other on Facebook," I explained, praying that the lie would hold up. Luckily, my mother had little use for social media, and so I knew I didn't have to worry about her commenting that she'd never seen this supposed "cousin" of mine interacting with me there. Not that I spent much time on Facebook, either, but she wouldn't know that.

"Oh," she said, then smiled. "Hi, Archie. I'm Elizabeth, Selena's mother, and this is my husband Tom."

Archie shook both their hands, saying he was happy to meet them. With those pleasantries out of the way, he apparently decided it was time to get to business.

"But perhaps we should see what your wedding planner is up to?" he said next, and I nodded, trying to ignore the flicker of confusion that passed over my mother's features. Most likely, she was trying to figure out why this long-lost cousin of mine would have anything to do with the layout for the ceremony and reception.

Before she could comment, I said hurriedly, "Yes, I want to make sure everything's going in the right place."

After waving at my mother and Tom, the three of us headed across the lawn to the spot where Victoria had paused with the foreman from the party-supply company. The rest of his team was still loitering at the foot of the porch steps, clearly just fine with hanging back until they got direct orders from their boss to get started.

As we approached, Victoria offered us all an apologetic smile. "Sorry about that," she said. "I just wanted to get the ball rolling." She stopped there, with an inquiring look over at Archie and back at me.

I made the introductions, glad to see that Archie appeared utterly composed as he shook Victoria's hand and told her he was very happy to meet her. Well, the man did have a Virgo stellium, after all. I didn't have to worry too much about him acting all lovestruck and stars in his eyes the way I might have with a Leo or a Sagittarius.

"This is where you're setting up the main party pavilion?" he asked politely, and Victoria nodded.

"Yes. This is the location where Selena wanted it to be placed, so we're just surveying the ground to double-check we're not going to hit any irrigation lines or anything like that."

Archie glanced over at the location, and then lifted his head as if to get a better look at the gardens in general. He'd told me he'd been here once before, long, long ago, but I doubted the scenery had changed much in the intervening years.

"Would it be possible to shift it about ten feet in that direction?" he said then, pointing at the spot in question. "I think from there, you'd have the mountains framed better above the trees at the edge of the garden."

Victoria looked impressed by this sugges-tion…or maybe she was just taking in the strong lines of his jaw and the elegant shape of his nose and liking what she saw. Archie definitely wasn't my type, but even I could admit he was an extremely good-looking man.

"You know, you're right," she said after a pause. "Selena, do you mind if we move the pavilion just a little?"

I glanced up at Calvin, whose shoulders lifted ever so slightly. As in most matters dealing with the wedding and its design, he was willing to let me make the big decisions.

"I think it's a great idea," I said. "As long as we're not going to be trampling any sprinklers or something. I know when Josie and I laid out the plans, we did our best to take all that into account."

The foreman nodded and headed over to walk the updated space and inspect it for any irrigation issues. After a few moments, he turned back towards our little group and gave us the thumbs-up.

"Well, that seems to settle it," Victoria said. "We'll put it over there."

A wave from their foreman, and the crew headed over to the truck to unload the pavilion. A little while after that, they started to erect the enormous structure.

And so went the rest of the day, with Archie inserting some pithily helpful comments and Victoria looking more and more impressed by the little tweaks he suggested. By the time we were ready to wrap it up a bit after four, the entire site had pretty much taken shape. All that was left to do would be to set up the flowers and lay out the table linens, but that wouldn't happen until the next morning.

"Is your friend Archie a party planner?" Victoria asked in an undertone as we headed back to the house, the men taking up the rear.

"No," I replied, doing my best to suppress a grin. "But he's always been a really organized person with an eye for detail. I suppose that's why he was so much help today."

Which he had been. I didn't know whether it was from a desire to impress Victoria or whether he was so happy to be human again that he was on his best behavior, but Archie had been pretty much a model citizen the whole day, with hardly a single snarky comment leaving his lips. That had to have been quite an effort, considering when we broke for lunch, we had to suffer the company of Tom's kids and their spouses. However, they also seemed to be behaving themselves...mostly. Their good behavior might simply have been the result of utter relief that there hadn't been any ghostly depredations that day or just a realization that they needed to at least attempt to be good guests, but either way, I'd take it.

Victoria absorbed my reply, expression thoughtful. Was she wondering why a supposed paragon like Archie was so obviously single?

I sure hoped so.

The party broke up after that, since the rehearsal dinner was in a few hours, and we all needed to get changed and ready for the much more formal gathering at the Gold Dust Casino's restaurant. I wished there was some way I could have included Archie in that particular get-together, but because he wasn't a member of the wedding party, it would have looked odd for him to be there.

"It's fine," he told me as I drove him back to his vacation rental. "That is, I'll be attending the wedding tomorrow. Asking for anything else would be a bit much, considering the way I turned up out of the blue."

I sent him a sideways glance. "You know," I remarked. "You're much nicer as a man than you were as a cat."

The cursed cat version of Archie might have gotten his hackles up at that remark. The man sitting in the passenger seat only looked thoughtful. "Well, having to use a litter box for seventy years would make anyone crabby."

About the only thing I could do was chuckle. "You have a point." I pulled up into the driveway and parked, then added, "Really, thank you so much for your help today. All those little tweaks you suggested are going to make the wedding so much better."

Was that a touch of pink I saw on his cheeks? Possibly—he was quite fair-skinned, and so reactions like that would be pretty obvious on him.

"Oh, it was nothing," he said. "Consider it my wedding gift to you and Calvin, since obviously, I won't be able to go out and buy you something."

"The only present I need is you there at the wedding," I said quite honestly. "Speaking of which, make sure you get in touch with Travis so he can get you there on time. The ceremony is at four, but we're going to start seating people at three-thirty."

"I'll be there," Archie promised, and then pushed the handle to open the car door.

Just as he was getting out, I added, "And Archie?"

He paused. "Yes?"

"I think Victoria was very impressed with you."

As I'd expected, he didn't reply, only closed the

car door and strode off toward the front porch of the house.

He was smiling, though.

Calvin had insisted on driving me to the rehearsal dinner, even though it was going pretty far out of his way to come into town to pick me up, only to turn around and head right back out to the casino. However, since I knew he'd been chafing a little at all the time we'd had to spend apart this week, I hadn't argued with him.

"You look amazing," he told me after I opened the door to let him in.

"Wait until tomorrow," I quipped, although I was glad he'd noticed that I'd gone to some extra effort this evening. I'd bought a pretty sleeveless purple dress, and had put on a little extra makeup and pulled my hair into an artfully messy up-do.

His dark eyes glinted. "I can't wait." But then he paused to look around the living room, his expression sober. "It's strange to think that Archie won't be your cat anymore."

"I know," I said, recalling my melancholy of earlier that morning. I was happy for Archie, but the apartment felt awfully empty now. "I was thinking maybe we could talk about getting a dog after we get back from our honeymoon."

"You want to switch teams?" Calvin asked in mock astonishment.

Because his mouth had quirked in amusement, I knew he was just pulling my leg. "I thought it would be nice to have a dog," I replied. "I grew up as an apartment dweller, remember? Dogs were pretty much off the table with the landlords we had."

At once, understanding flashed across his face, and he reached over and pulled me into a hug. Warm breath moved across the top of my head as he said, "Of course you can have a dog. You can have a whole sled team of dogs if you want. It's not like there isn't plenty of room at the house."

That was true. The home we would soon share was much bigger than my apartment, a sprawling three thousand feet or so of living space, and that didn't even take into account the big five-acre plot of land it sat on.

"I was thinking maybe one small dog to start," I told him. "No need to get crazy."

His fingers brushed a stray lock of hair away from my face. "What if I want to get crazy with you?"

I grinned, and pulled away just enough so I could gaze up into his face. "Save it for the wedding night, loverboy."

He returned the smile, his dark eyes crinkling with amusement. "If I must. But now, we should probably get going. I doubt we'd hear the end of it if we were late for our own rehearsal dinner."

"Probably not," I agreed. Calvin's and my mothers were very different people, but they were both pretty big on punctuality. "Let me grab my purse."

We headed out after that, driving Calvin's police-issue Durango over to the casino restaurant. Victoria was already there, as I'd expected, but otherwise, Calvin and I were the first to arrive.

For just a second, a hint of disappointment flickered across her face as she saw us walk in, but then a professional smile spread across her lips. "Hi, there," she said. "Getting excited?"

"Very," I replied, even if I wondered whether that ghost of regret I'd glimpsed was her wishing we'd brought Archie with us, even if he really had no reason to attend the rehearsal dinner. "I think seeing everything getting set up this afternoon really brought home how close it all is."

"And it's going to look great," Calvin put in. "Thanks so much for stepping in at the last minute and making sure it all works out the way we'd planned."

"That's what I'm here for," she said. Her gaze moved past us to the entrance to the private dining room we'd rented for the evening. "It looks like everyone else is starting to arrive."

Yes, there were my mother and Tom, and behind them Nick and Madison and their spouses. Right on their heels were Calvin's parents, and then I saw Hazel and Chuck bringing up the rear. Chuck had very graciously agreed to officiate, since he'd gotten one of those Universal Life Church ordinations a few years back to perform his parents' vow renewal for their fiftieth wedding anniversary.

Although Terry Woodrow and her husband Brett hadn't yet shown up, I figured we had enough of a quorum to go ahead and start the proceedings. And just as we were shuffling to get into our places, Terry appeared, falling into line behind Hazel and the rest of the bridesmaids.

Honestly, I wasn't having an elaborate ceremony, so there wasn't all that much to rehearse. Still, it was nice to do a couple of walk-throughs, if only to solidify for everyone what was expected of them. Afterward, we had a mellow dinner, with everyone chatting like old friends, and so the evening passed quickly enough.

My mother wanted everyone to come back to the house for a drink after dinner, and since it was still early, we all agreed—well, except for Victoria, who said she wanted to go over her lists one last time, and Terry and Brett, who'd left their two small children at home with a babysitter and needed to get back as soon as they could. But after we'd parked and all started walking up the flag-stone path to the front door, Calvin paused, brows drawing together as he stared across the lawn where the pavilion had been set up.

Or rather, where it used to be set up. I stopped next to him and stared in consternation at the empty expanse of grass, even as a sinking feeling enveloped me.

"Where's the pavilion?" my mother said, staring in the same direction we were.

"It's gone," I replied, my tone flat.

"No, wait," Calvin said, then pointed. In the darkness, it was hard to make out a lot of details, but then I detected a big white blur somewhere at the edges of my vision, a blur I guessed was the pavilion, unassembled and tossed in a heap.

It looked like Susanna was up to her old tricks.

Mouth set in anger, I snapped, "All right—that does it!"

And I began marching toward the door. That troublesome ghost and I were going to have it out, once and for all.

"What are you going to do?" Calvin asked, hurrying to catch up with me. The rest of our group followed, Tom trying to keep pace as well, since he needed to unlock the front door.

"I'm going to make her stop," I announced.

"No matter what it takes."

14

Toys in the Attic

"SUSANNA CAROLINE BIGELOW!" I SHOUTED from the foot of the stairs. My voice floated upward through the stairwell, bouncing off the woodwork and sounding like a chorus of mocking echoes.

No reply…which was about what I'd expected.

Everyone had gathered nearby, most of them wearing worried expressions, although Tom's son Nick looked more like he was just enjoying the show rather than feeling personally involved in any of this.

Well, he should feel involved. Now that Susannah had taken out her ire on the pavilions, there was no telling where she'd focus her dubious attention next.

And then, for just the briefest moment, she

popped into existence on the landing. "You *did* tell me not to touch anything in the house," she called down to me, as everyone—Nick included—stared at her with a mixture of consternation and disbelief. "And I didn't."

"That's splitting some pretty small hairs," I retorted

I was deprived of the chance to say anything more, though, because she disappeared just as quickly as she'd come. Hands planted on my hips, I glared at the spot she'd occupied just a second earlier.

"Let it go, Selena," Calvin said quietly, ignoring the worried murmurs of our companions. "My father and I can get a bunch of people to come over tomorrow morning and set everything to rights. I've noticed your ghost seems to create the most mischief at night, so I don't think she's going to cause a problem in broad daylight."

One could only hope. However, I had to believe that the presence of a bunch of burly San Ramon Apache on the property would probably provide a dampening effect.

Problem was, I knew I wouldn't be able to relax for a single moment, never knowing what mischief the ghost might try next to throw a monkey wrench into the proceedings. Was that how I wanted to spend my wedding day, never letting my guard down?

Hell, no.

The only real way to get a ghost to stop haunting a place was to puzzle out the cause for the haunting and then do whatever was necessary to set it right. And although I'd done my darnedest to discover what tragedy had kept Susanna Bigelow anchored to the house where she'd grown up, so far all those efforts had turned up a big fat zero.

Except….

My gaze strayed upward. Not toward the landing where she'd last appeared, but much farther up, all the way to the enormous attic that occupied the third floor of the mansion. I couldn't see it from where I stood, of course, and yet I remembered what it had looked like when I first came to do a tour of their new purchase with my mother and Tom, how the cavernous space had been filled with boxes of all sorts of things, from vintage clothing to Christmas decorations. Hank and Nora Anders had left everything behind…but what if the people they'd bought the house from had also left their castoffs there as well? What if some of those boxes and trunks dated all the way back to Susanna Bigelow's tenure in the house?

Well, there was only one way to find out.

"I need to check on something," I said, and began to climb the steps. At once, Calvin followed, my mother straggling a little behind, while the rest of the wedding party hovered around the foot of the stairs, clearly unsure as to what they should do next.

"Check on what?" my mother asked. "Selena, just let it go. You're getting married tomorrow, and Calvin's right. We'll get help to put everything back together. There's no need to run yourself ragged the night before your big day."

"Mom, I might not have a 'big day' if I don't get this handled," I said over my shoulder, since I wasn't about to stop steaming my way up the stairs.

"I think you're being melodramatic—"

Calvin cut in there, but gently. "Elizabeth, Selena has very good instincts about this sort of thing. If she thinks she needs to take care of it now, we have to let her." By that point, we'd reached the second floor, and he paused for a second to send a searching glance in my direction. "Do you want us to stay here?"

Oh, how I loved that man of mine. Sometimes he knew me better than I knew myself.

"Yes, please," I replied. "I think the more people who are up in the attic, scattering their energies around, the less chance I'll be able to home in on what I have to do."

My mother still looked dubious, but at least she didn't offer any further protests beyond saying, "Try not to stay up there too long."

"I'll do my best," I replied. Since I had absolutely no idea how long any of this was going to take, I couldn't say much beyond that.

But apparently, it was enough, because after Calvin reached out and gave my hand a reassuring squeeze, the two of them turned around and headed down the stairs.

Thank the Goddess.

Mouth set, I continued to the end of the hall, where the narrow staircase that led to the attic was located. Once upon a time, it would have been used by the home's servants, who slept on the third floor of the house. Somewhere along the way, however, the servants' quarters had been converted to an attic storage space where all the flotsam and jetsam of the house tended to end up.

I climbed the stairs, turning on lights as I went. Yes, I knew that nothing evil lurked here—even Susanna was just a pain in the neck, and not a malignant force—but having all the lights blazing helped to reassure me, if nothing else.

When I entered the attic, it looked pretty much the same as it had the last time I'd been here. True, there was no longer a large flowered chamber pot sitting in the middle of the space to catch drips, since the leak in the roof had been repaired months ago. Otherwise, though, I didn't think anything had been moved, or worse, thrown out altogether.

Hands on my hips, I surveyed the room. It was hot up here, since even though the house had long ago been converted to forced heat and air, Nora and Hank obviously hadn't bothered to extend the ductwork into the attic.

Good thing I'd put my hair up for the rehearsal dinner.

However, I wasn't really dressed for rooting around in an attic space, not in my silk dress and high-heeled sandals.

Since I wasn't about to go home and change, I'd just have to suck it up.

Right away, I thought I could ignore the cardboard boxes filled with holiday decorations and discarded clothing. They were of a much more recent vintage than the clothes Susanna Bigelow wore, and so I doubted I'd find anything of hers in any of them.

The trunks and antique furniture were a different story, however. Some of the pieces were nice enough that they should have been polished up and sold in an antique store, and for all I knew, that was what my mother planned to do with them eventually. Right now, though, I thought any of those various dressers and armoires could be a hiding place for Susanna's former belongings.

A large steamer trunk rested on the floor nearby, and so I figured I'd look in there first. However, while it did include some elegant vintage pieces, including an exquisite beaded dress that I wanted to take home with me, there was absolutely nothing of a personal nature in there, not even embroidered initials on the collar of a blouse.

All right, time to move on.

The next few trunks I examined contained much the same sort of thing, except the gowns seemed even older, pieces with impossibly tiny waists and the ruching and ruffling I thought was typical of dresses from around the turn of the last century. Alice Bigelow's things, maybe, put up here after styles changed…or after she'd had a couple of kids and could no longer fit into those wasp-waisted gowns.

More trunks, more clothes, and still nothing.

All right. Time to move on to the furniture.

I rooted around in several dressers and didn't get anything for my trouble except a couple of splinters. While part of me wanted to give up and head downstairs so I could beg a pair of tweezers and some hydrogen peroxide from my mother, I told myself I was made of tougher stuff than that. I could attend to the necessary first aid after I was done here. At least I'd gotten a gel manicure during my spa afternoon the day before, and so I didn't need to worry too much about destroying my nails on the eve of my wedding.

Wedged way at the far end of the attic was a

pretty suite of furniture, what appeared to be walnut with elegant carving and marble tops. Seeing it, my heart began to beat a little faster.

That looked exactly like the kind of set that might have once resided in Susanna Bigelow's bedroom.

Still, I told myself not to get my hopes up. After all, I'd just spent at least an hour going through all sorts of miscellaneous junk. What made me think I'd find what I needed here?

Well, other than the all-too-familiar sensation in my gut that told me I was on the right track.

However, after digging through the highboy and the large chest of drawers and two bedside tables, I began to think maybe my gut instinct wasn't all it was cracked up to be. There didn't seem to be anything here at all.

Then I noticed a little table shoved into the corner, a piece that I guessed had once been a vanity, since it obviously had been constructed to hold a mirror between its two posts, a mirror that had probably been broken decades earlier, as it didn't seem to be anywhere around.

Just the sort of place to hide love letters, or maybe a diary?

Maybe, even though I told myself that even if Susanna Bigelow had hidden such things in there, they had to have been removed decades earlier.

Or maybe not. It seemed plausible enough to

me that the furniture had been moved hastily out of her room after her death, and so it was entirely possible no one had looked inside the vanity at all.

Well, I was about to.

I went over to the little table and opened one of the drawers. A faint scent of lemon verbena drifted out as I did so, but the drawer was completely empty.

Had I imagined that perfume, or was Susanna lurking somewhere nearby, just waiting to pounce?

Doing my best to ignore the prickly feeling on the back of my neck that particular thought had given me, I turned my attention to the other drawer. When I tried to pull it open, however, it only moved a fraction of an inch.

Something appeared to be jammed in there.

I bent down and peered inside but couldn't see much. Luckily, I'd set my purse on the floor near the entrance to the attic when I first came up here, so I hurried over, dug out my phone, and then went back to the little vanity so I could shine the phone's flashlight inside.

Sure enough, a slim volume of some sort had slipped out of position so it was wedged in place, preventing me from getting the drawer to pull all the way out.

Jackpot.

Now that I could see what was going on, it

wasn't too difficult to reach inside, fumble around a bit, and then dislodge the book. It fell to the bottom of the drawer with a faint thud.

Smiling, I turned off the flashlight function and set my phone down on top of the table, then reached in and drew out the book. It was covered in dark brown leather and had a fanciful floral framework stamped in gold. Inside that frame was a single word.

Diary.

"Put that back!"

I turned to see Susanna Bigelow standing a few feet away, hands planted on her hips and anger shooting from her forget-me-not eyes.

"What, this?" I said, hefting the book in one hand.

She dived for me, but since she was an incorporeal being, all she did was pass right through, sending an odd little shudder through my body at the icy sensation. No doubt she achieved all her poltergeist mischief through sheer force of will and not by actual physical contact.

It was still a little unnerving, though.

"That's private!" she snapped.

Under most circumstances, I would have respected her wishes. However, since she seemed bound and determined to disrupt my wedding in any way possible, she hadn't left me much choice.

That didn't mean I couldn't try bargaining.

"Okay," I said, still maintaining a death grip on the diary just in case she tried anything funny. "I won't read this if you'll tell me what's inside."

She looked aghast. "I can't do that!"

"Well, then," I said calmly, and opened the little book. On the flyleaf was written the words, *The Diary of Susanna Caroline Bigelow, 1916.* Clearly, she'd started writing in the diary several years before whatever calamitous events occurred that had caused her to lose her life.

"No!" She dived for me again, but, just like the last time, she didn't accomplish much beyond sending another funny little chill down my spine.

This was getting ridiculous.

After she stamped her foot and sent me a glare of impotent rage, though, she disappeared.

Had she realized trying to do anything physical to me was an exercise in futility?

It definitely looked that way.

I returned my attention to the diary. The first thirty or forty pages were full of commonplace observations—comments on new dresses, or what she'd had for dinner, or a new set of books that had been shipped all the way from New York. After that, however, the tone changed drastically.

Rudolfo and I met again in the garden, Susanna had written. *It is so tiresome to sneak around in such a way, but both his family and mine would certainly be furious if they discovered our attachment. My father, of course, would think a Mexican boy far beneath me, and Rudolfo's father could only be angry about his son forming an attraction to someone whose family would never agree to the match. But we must see each other when we can, and form our plans. I want to run far, far away from here—Rudolfo thinks that we should be able to start over in Los Angeles. No one would know us there, and I would become Susanna Monsalvo and leave Globe and all its irksome restrictions behind.*

The entry ended there, and I paused. So, Susanna had been romantically involved with a boy of Mexican descent? I supposed back in her day, such a relationship would have created quite a scandal, with the lines between ethnicities so much more sharply drawn than they were today.

Something must have gone horribly wrong.

But what?

I flipped through the pages, scanning quickly past accounts of Susanna and Rudolfo's assignations, their plans to run away to California.

And then, on a tear-splotched page, the last one in the journal that contained an entry, I found the words that sent another chill down my spine.

All is lost, she wrote. *We have been discovered, and Father went into a towering rage and threatened to shoot Rudolfo if he ever set foot on the property again. He has locked me in my room and sworn that I may not come out again until I agree to marry a man of his choosing. And Samuel is of no help, because he is also horrified that a Bigelow would dally with someone he thinks is so far beneath us.*

I have no recourse, nothing left. But I will have the last laugh. They think they've trapped me here, but I know I can escape. Just a single moment of pain, just one moment in the air, and then I will be gone from this life. I'll wait in the hereafter until Rudolfo can come to me.

Very gently, I closed the book. Well, now I knew why Susanna lingered in this place.

I'll wait in the hereafter until Rudolfo can come to me.

Only, he hadn't come. No, he'd left her caught between two worlds, eternally pining for someone who would never appear.

Maybe that was why she'd said "gone" the first time I encountered her. She hadn't been talking about herself, but the man she'd loved, the man she'd been waiting for all those long, lonely years.

And while I hated to acknowledge that such blind prejudice even existed, I guessed the reason why all mention of Susanna Bigelow had been erased from existence was that her family couldn't acknowledge how their only daughter had died by her own hand. Most likely, it hadn't taken much effort to make the parish priest remove her name from the baptismal register, or to ensure that no one spoke of her ever again.

Poor Susanna. No wonder she'd tried so hard to stop my wedding—she couldn't bear to see someone happily married on the grounds of the very house where she'd taken her life.

Was there any way to fix this?

As soon as that despairing thought crossed my mind, however, another notion struck me. What Susanna needed was closure. What if I could dig up some information about Rudolfo, something that would set her mind at ease and let her know it was all right to move on from this plane?

Sure, I thought next. *You can just go hack a bunch of databases with your nonexistent computing skills and find exactly what you need, all in the next twelve hours.*

Okay, when I put it that way....

Then again, I had to believe that Rudolfo Monsalvo wasn't exactly a common name. I didn't have the computer expertise to discover what had happened to him, but I didn't need to. No, I had Calvin and the entire San Ramon police department...and police had access to databases full of information that a civilian like me would normally never be able to view.

That seemed to settle it. Gently, I put the diary back in the drawer where I'd found it—I'd already violated Susanna's privacy enough, and didn't see the need to share her journal with anyone else—and then went over to retrieve my bag and hurry down the stairs as quickly as my high-heeled sandals would let me.

Calvin and Tom and my mother were all sitting in the front salon, talking quietly, although it looked as if everyone else had gone to bed.

Good. I really hadn't been looking forward to explaining this whole situation in front of Tom's kids.

"I found something," I said as I paused in the entry to the salon and they all gazed at me with expectant eyes. "Susanna Bigelow committed suicide when her father wouldn't let her marry a local Mexican boy. He threatened to shoot the poor kid." I paused there, and looked over at my fiancé. "Calvin, I know it's asking a lot, but is there someone at the station who could do a search on Rudolfo Monsalvo for me? I need to find out what happened to him."

To my relief, Calvin nodded, then rose from the chair where he'd been sitting and came over to take my hand and give it a reassuring squeeze. "You're in luck. Josh—my deputy who dug up the info on Miriam Jacobsen's fake shell company—is on duty tonight. If anyone can find what you need, it's him. I'll text him right now."

While Calvin got out his phone and started

typing out a text, my mother said, "It's tragic about that poor girl, Selena, but you really need to let this go. It's almost eleven o'clock!"

I shook my head. "I can't do that, Mom. I have to get Susanna the closure she needs, or she's going to continue to disrupt everything. And she's probably extra pissed off now that I went through her diary."

Her mouth pursed, but my mother didn't have a chance to reply before Calvin said, "Josh is on it. I gave him your number so he can text you directly."

I sent him a grateful look, and glanced back over at my mother. "Okay, that's being handled. But I promise I'll have Calvin take me to the apartment now, and I promise I'll try to get some sleep."

For a moment, she didn't reply, only watched me carefully, as though to find the hidden gotcha in those words. But then she gave a weary lift of her shoulders. "All right. Get some rest."

She didn't add, *You have a big day tomorrow,* but I heard the words in my head anyway.

"I'll be over at one," I said, which was the time when the hairstylists and makeup artists were due to arrive. Since Calvin wasn't supposed to see me the day of the wedding, and my mother would have been horrified if I drove myself over to the mansion, Hazel and Chuck were planning to drop by the apartment and pick me up.

After that, we said goodbye, and Calvin and I headed out, then climbed into the Durango. As he was pulling out of the driveway, he said, "I suppose it's too much to ask you not to act on whatever information Josh digs up."

"Probably," I said with a grin. "Like I said to my mom, I've got to get this straightened out, or all hell could break loose tomorrow."

He let out a resigned breath. "All right. You know what you're doing. Just…be careful."

"Aren't I always?"

That rhetorical question got me a shake of the head, although he knew better than to comment that my amateur sleuthing had landed me in hot water on more than one occasion. Rather than answer directly, he said, "Oh, and I got in touch with my father and let him know what happened with the reception tents. He promised a whole crew of cousins and friends to show up tomorrow at nine to get everything set back up. And I texted Victoria and Archie, too, since we really need them there to make sure all the pavilions are put in the right places."

Thank the Goddess for Calvin Standingbear. I'd been so focused on halting Susanna's rampage that I hadn't even stopped to think that Victoria and Archie would need to be involved in the reconstruction efforts if we wanted the site setup to mirror what they'd done earlier that day.

"What did they say?"

"Victoria was horrified, but glad to hear my dad had corralled a bunch of Standingbears to put everything back together," Calvin said. "And Archie said he wasn't surprised, but he'd be at the house at nine." A pause, and he added with a grin, "I never thought I'd be sharing texts with your cat."

"He's not a cat anymore," I said, somewhat severely, but Calvin's smile didn't fade.

"I know, but it's probably going to take me a while to stop thinking of him that way. He seems to have grasped the use of a phone pretty easily."

"He's watched me plenty of times," I replied, which was only the truth. Also, he had the manual that came with the phone, and I had no doubt he'd read it cover to cover. Archie was just like that. Still, I was glad to hear he seemed to be managing that necessity of life in the twenty-first century without too many problems.

We pulled into one of the spaces behind my building, and Calvin turned off the engine. "It's going to be okay," he said, reaching over so he could gently squeeze my hand.

The pressure of his fingers against mine was infinitely reassuring. With Calvin around, it was hard to believe everything wouldn't turn out just fine in the end. And as much as I wanted him to come upstairs with me, I knew he needed to get his sleep. I didn't have to do much of anything except be ready to head out a little before one, but he would probably be on site at nine in the morning with the rest of his family, doing what needed to be done to ensure everything was ready to give the two of us our perfect day.

Instead of ending the evening the way I really wanted, Calvin and I settled for a long, lingering kiss, and then he waited in his Durango, watching to make sure I got inside safely and locked the door behind me. As I set the deadbolt, I heard the SUV's engine start up again, followed by the sound of him backing out.

A small sigh escaped my lips, but I made myself walk up the stairs to my apartment, then unlocked the door and let myself in. Once again, I was struck by how empty it felt with Archie gone.

But I needed to be happy for him…and I needed to focus on the task at hand.

Which at the moment was pretty much sitting around and waiting to hear from Josh. One part of my mind told me I should pack it in and get ready for bed, but once again, that little flutter somewhere in my gut advised me that probably wasn't a good idea.

So, I went into the kitchen and got some water heating, since I figured I could have a cup of green tea to occupy myself for a bit. It would provide just enough caffeine to help me feel a bit perkier, but not so much that I'd have to worry about tossing and turning all night when I was supposed to be getting my beauty sleep.

And I hadn't been sitting on the couch, sipping the tea, for more than five or so minutes before my phone pinged.

I could think of only one person who'd be texting me at that hour, now a little past eleven-thirty.

Hoping for just such a text, I'd left my phone within easy reach on the coffee table. I practically lunged for it with my free hand, barely avoiding spilling some of my tea in the process.

Sure enough, the text was from Calvin's deputy. *Found this,* he said. *The dates line up. I hope it's your guy. And congrats on the wedding!*

Attached to the message was what looked like a screen shot from an obituary. It was dated March 21, 1979.

Rudolfo Monsalvo is survived by his brother Armando, sisters Lucinda and Maria, and numerous nephews, nieces, and grand-nephews and nieces. A beloved brother and uncle, he will be mourned by the community, and by the employees at the nursery he established in 1925. Requiescat in pace.

No mention of a wife or children.

Had he mourned the loss of Susanna Bigelow until the day he died? I didn't want to assign intentions without having more facts on hand, but it sure sounded that way.

And in that case….

I texted back, *Thank you SO much, Josh! This is exactly what I was looking for!*

You're welcome, he replied. *Now, go to sleep.*

I chuckled. Yes, I hoped that sleep was in my near future, but I had something else to do first.

Time to get Susanna Bigelow to finally relinquish her hold on this earth.

15

Happily Ever After

I HURRIED DOWN THE HALL TO MY OFFICE, then turned on the light and immediately headed for the bookcase shelf where my crystal ball resided. After removing the embroidered cloth that covered it and setting it on my altar, I said, "Grandma Ellen, are you there? It's urgent!"

No reply at first, but then she appeared in a blink out of nowhere, without the misty veil that usually heralded her arrival. "Selena, what's going on?" she asked, worry flitting across her features. "Why aren't you in bed? You're getting married tomorrow, you know."

If one more person told me that….

Somehow, I managed to avoid an epic eye roll. "Yes, I know. But I need to get something handled first." I stopped there, wondering how best to phrase the request I was about to make. It certainly wasn't anything I'd asked of my grandmother before, and something I didn't even know was possible or not.

But desperate times called for desperate measures, and I was nothing if not desperate.

"I need you to reach out to a certain spirit," I told her. "I need you to find someone called Rudolfo Monsalvo, a man who died in 1979. He left behind someone grieving and unable to move on, and I was hoping that if I could talk to him, I could let her know he died still loving her. If she realizes he's there in the afterlife, waiting for her, then she won't have any reason to cling to an existence here."

My grandmother listened to this plea with an expression of growing consternation on her face. "Selena, you know it doesn't necessarily work like that. There's every possibility that this Rudolfo Monsalvo has already returned to your plane to live out another existence and learn another lesson."

"I know that," I replied. Even as I'd made the request, I'd realized what a long shot it was. Still, I had to try—and I needed my grandmother's help for that.

For a second or two, she didn't say anything. Her mouth compressed—a mouth wearing her favorite "Cherries in the Snow" lipstick from Revlon—and then she nodded, albeit reluctantly.

"I'll do what I can," she said. "That's all I can promise—I don't even know if he's here, and it might take me some time to find him."

Again, I didn't have much choice. I could, however, allow myself to be cheered slightly that at least she hadn't given me a flat refusal. As for the rest, I'd just have to leave it up to fate. So far, it hadn't steered me wrong.

In the meantime, though, I'd do what I could to hedge my bets. Even if I couldn't hear directly from Rudolfo, I could at least go back to the mansion and do my best to let Susanna know that the man she'd loved had loved her back just as fiercely, and she was only hurting herself by remaining here.

"Thanks, Grandma Ellen," I said. "I just know this is going to work."

I'd said those words more to cheer myself up than because I truly believed them, but she didn't try to deflate my hopes, only murmured, "I'll see what I can do," before disappearing.

Okay. I had my grandmother on the case, but I had my own work to do.

Good thing I hadn't yielded to that impulse to get into my jammies.

After returning my phone to my purse, I

headed out. At that time of night, Globe was dead quiet, even though it was a Friday evening. Farther down Broad Street, I had to assume that things were still jumping at the Drift Inn, a bar frequented by bikers and other rough types I probably wouldn't want to invite to Sunday dinner, but they were far enough away I couldn't hear much of anything.

Similarly, the streets were empty as I made my way across town and then up the winding hillside road that led to the Bigelow mansion. I did my best not to give in to my impulse to speed, even though it was hard to drive sedately.

Susanna's waited a hundred years, I reminded myself. *She can wait a few minutes more.*

I parked some distance from the garage—I didn't want even the faintest sound of my car's passage to make its way up to the house. True, the place was closed up tight, since my mother kept the A/C running around the clock, but still, no point in taking any chances. I could only imagine her reaction if she discovered me roaming around the property at midnight the day before my wedding.

Because I'd driven over to the mansion, I'd been aware of a mounting urge to not go to the house itself, but to go somewhere on the grounds instead. It was true that Susanna didn't seem to inhabit her former home full-time, and instead must have had some other place nearby where she went to ground.

In fact, I pulled out the little garnet pendulum that I kept in an inner pocket of my purse against emergencies such as this, and allowed it to guide me once I emerged from the car. It swung in a straight arc back and forth, drawing me past the wide lawn where the pavilions would be set up again the next morning, through the rose gardens where the scent of the flowers' perfume on the warm night air was nearly suffocating, and out into a half-wild area planted with meadow grass and a variety of trees, all the way to nearly the edge of the property, where a large sycamore shaded the low stone wall that marked the border of the gardens.

Now the pendulum swung back and forth so fiercely, I had to hold it with a grip of iron so it wouldn't go flying right out of my hand. At the same time, a misty figure slowly resolved itself in front of me.

Susanna.

"So, you found me," she said, sounding resigned.

"I figured you had to be around somewhere," I replied. My gaze moved from her to the large flat rock that was half concealed among the sycamore's roots.

She looked down at the rock as well, her

expression almost wistful. "This is where they buried me. No question of me getting to occupy the family mausoleum, after all."

Right. As someone who'd died by her own hand, she wouldn't have been allowed to be buried in the small, quaint graveyard attached to St. Ignatius. I had to hope that particular barbaric practice had been abandoned during the intervening years, but since I wasn't Catholic, I didn't know for sure.

"It's a beautiful spot," I told her. "I think I'd rather be out here with the wind and the trees than stuck in a stuffy mausoleum anyway."

A very faint nod, and then she said, "I suppose you've come here to tell me to stop."

"Well, I think you should," I said frankly. "But I also wanted to let you know I found out something about Rudolfo. He passed away more than forty years ago, and lived to be almost eighty. In all that time, though, he never married. I have to believe he never stopped loving you."

Susanna had already been standing quite still, but after that revelation, it looked as though she might as well have been carved from stone. For just a second, hope flared in her eyes, hope I could see even in the faint light from the crescent moon and the desert stars overhead.

Then it faded, and she shook her head. "You're only telling me what you think I want to hear."

And all right, I did believe Susanna would have wanted to know that her one true love had never abandoned her for someone else. At the same time, though, I wouldn't have told her what I believed if I hadn't also thought it was the truth.

"No, I'm not," I replied. "I—"

But I broke off there, because I realized Susanna and I weren't alone. Someone was approaching through the shimmering night-lit grass, a tall man with black hair combed straight back from his proud-boned face, a man I realized couldn't have been much older than Susanna herself. His white shirt with the rolled-up sleeves could have been from almost any era, but those pleated pants held up by suspenders were the sort of thing that hadn't been in style for decades.

She let out an incoherent little cry and ran to him. He spread out his arms, and she let herself be folded into a fierce embrace.

No living human could hug a ghost like that. Which meant…

…which meant he was a ghost as well.

Of course he was. There was only one person in the world Susanna would have hugged like that.

"Hi, Rudolfo," I said, hoping I sounded casual, as if I reunited ghosts every day. Inside, though…inside, a big knot of unshed tears tightened in my chest.

No crying, though. I didn't want Calvin to have a puffy-eyed bride.

Rudolfo looked past the top of Susanna's head and smiled at me, but then he immediately glanced back down at her. "I'm sorry it took me so long to find you, my love," he said. "Now that I'm here, though, will you come back with me?"

For just a second, she hesitated, her gaze moving around the dark gardens that surrounded us on all sides. Maybe she was still afraid to move on, still wasn't sure if she could let herself leave the only existence she'd ever known.

But then she nodded. "I'm ready, dearest. Let's go."

He released her, but only so he could take her hand in his and lead her away from the sycamore tree, away from the place her family had buried her in shame. As they walked, they grew more and more transparent, until I knew I was completely alone.

"Thanks, Grandma Ellen," I murmured.

For just a moment, I stood there in the moon-light and the starlight, feeling the jangly energy that had accompanied Susanna's ghost begin to dissipate. Maybe one very faint whiff of lemon verbena, and then it was gone as well.

Time to go home. As everyone had been so fond of telling me, I was getting married tomorrow.

I eyed my reflection critically, but either the makeup artist Josie and I had hired was just that good, or I really hadn't suffered any ill effects from my midnight outing the evening before. True, I'd been in bed by twelve-thirty and had slept like the dead until almost nine, but still.

"Everything all right?" the makeup artist, whose name was Desirée, asked me with some trepidation. She was one of those effortlessly glamorous women whose cat-eye liner was on point and who looked as though they'd been born wearing Russian Red lipstick and perfect eyelashes.

"Everything's fine," I assured her. "And these magnetic lashes are awesome. They feel like they aren't going anywhere."

"They aren't," she assured me. "No matter how windy it gets."

A peek out the window told me the day was breezy, as most days in Arizona seemed to be, but I didn't think I needed to worry about gale-force winds or anything like that. And I'd been reassured to see that the forecasts were holding, and that temperatures promised to top out around eighty-five degrees under a mostly sunny sky.

Calvin and I had definitely been blessed with a perfect day for the wedding.

"Fifteen minutes," Victoria said, popping her head into the secondary salon the bridal party had been using for their preparations. Good thing that the Bigelow mansion's electrical system had been completely updated, or no doubt it would have been pushed to the breaking point by all those makeup mirrors and curling irons.

"Getting into my gown now," I assured her. And since it was a simple enough dress, not some enormous construct with a complicated bustle or a row of fifty teeny-tiny satin-covered buttons up the back, I knew that wouldn't take very long.

"Perfect," she replied. "I'll be waiting at the door for you."

Hazel, Madison, Terry and Staci were already dressed and ready to go. Tom's daughter and daughter-in-law headed out first, to my great relief, followed by Terry soon afterward, and then my mother and my best friend gingerly helped me into my dress, making sure that nothing touched the low, artfully messy bun at the back of my neck, or the long, loose curls that framed my face.

I picked up the flowered crown and set it on my head, then turned around. At once, Hazel clasped her hands together, and my mother's big blue eyes teared up.

"Oh, you look so beautiful," she sighed, and I sent her a grateful smile.

"Thanks, Mom," I replied, then added quickly, "but don't start crying yet. You should at least wait until I'm walking down the aisle."

She shook her head, but it seemed my comment had had the intended effect and had staved off the threatened waterworks, because she did look a little less blurry.

"I'm fine," she said, although she did wave her hands on either side of her eyes for a moment to dispel any lingering tears, just to be safe. Then she came over to me and wrapped her fingers around mine. "This is your day, my darling. Now, go and enjoy it."

Before I could reply, she'd hurried out, most likely headed for her seat in the front row of chairs at the ceremony site. And how beautiful everything had looked when I arrived that afternoon—Calvin and his cousins had painstakingly reconstructed and relocated all the tents, and Victoria's moving team had already set out all the tables and chairs in the main reception pavilion. Her assistant Melanie, who'd driven in from Scottsdale for the day, had been in the process of tying ribbons in all shades of the rainbow to the backs of the those chairs when I got to the site, but I could still tell it was going to be gorgeous when everything was done.

As promised, Victoria was waiting for me

when I emerged onto the porch through a side door, standing in the lee of the house so no one could see me before I got to the ceremony site and began my walk down the aisle. She was looking very beautiful as well, in an understated silk shantung sheath in a soft blush color, with pearls at her ears and her throat and nude sling-backs on her feet.

"Ready?" she asked, and I nodded.

After all, I'd been ready to marry Calvin Standingbear for months. This was just a formality and nothing more.

A very complicated, very pretty formality, but still.

She guided me around to the front of the porch, where Tom stood at the top of the steps, very dapper in a dark suit with a deep rose silk tie. His eyes lit up at the sight of me in my gown, and he offered me his arm.

I took it, realizing in that moment that this was really going to happen, that no supernatural intervention was going to prevent the ceremony from going off without a hitch. Susanna had finally moved on, and I knew I had nothing to worry about from her.

Even so, a little flutter in my stomach told me I wasn't quite as cool and composed as I thought. I waited with Tom while my bridesmaids made their way down the aisle, accompanied by a mix of

Calvin's brothers and cousins, until at last the music shifted to "Spring" from Vivaldi's *Four Seasons,* and I knew it was time for me to take that long walk.

Down I went, past the rows and rows of chairs filled with friends from Globe—I spied Josie's smiling face, and her nephew Brett next to her, and Rosa from Olamendi's and even Henry Lewis, the eternally disapproving police chief and his wife Joyce, whose candles I sold in my store. And Maisie Hoskins all the way from L.A., and others from my Los Angeles life as well: Brenda Stein, a fellow psychic, and Natalie Figueroa and Jules Miller, former clients who'd remained friends. On the other side of the aisle were Calvin's friends and family, all of them San Ramon Apache…and quite a few looking a little uncomfortable in their suits and pretty cocktail dresses.

There was Chuck, too, standing at the altar and also seeming a bit stiff in his dress suit and tie…although I noticed a pair of well-polished cowboy boots peeking out from beneath his crisp slacks and had to keep myself from cracking a grin.

But then I saw Calvin, sleek black hair pulled back into a ponytail holder accented with turquoise, his tie a deep teal to coordinate, and I couldn't see anyone else, couldn't see anything except those gorgeous dark eyes as they met mine and held.

Everything after that was sort of a blur, although I luckily didn't forget the words to our vow, those simple few sentences we'd come up with together.

I promise to give you the best of myself and to ask of you no more than you can give....

And then it was time for him to kiss me, and time for the world to spin around as I tasted his wonderful mouth and realized that was my husband's mouth, that we'd been joined in a bond much, much stronger than the laws that now made us legally husband and wife.

We walked down the aisle hand in hand, with everyone standing and clapping on either side. Some enterprising Standingbear children had scooped up the silk flower petals that lined the aisle and were tossing them into the air and laughing, and Calvin and I laughed as well as petals floated around us in a riot of color.

Had I ever been this happy?

I couldn't be sure, but I didn't think so.

The two of us had promised each other early on that this would first and foremost be the best party ever, and so there wasn't anything terribly formal about the reception that followed. No line to greet our guests, no head table—the two of us sat at our little "sweetheart" table in the big pavilion and toasted each other with some fabulous cabernet, and then had a wonderful meal of filet mignon and probably the best herb-roasted potatoes I'd ever eaten. A small interval to wander and mingle and thank people for coming, and after that cake and champagne.

By that point, I was feeling a little swimmy, although whether that was from all the wine and bubbly or just the euphoric high of knowing that we'd pulled off the entire thing despite Susanna's interference, I didn't know for sure. And that was why I had to blink at the entirely unexpected sight of Archie leading Victoria out to the dance floor when the band started playing "The Way You Look Tonight"—I'd purposely chosen mostly old standards for the reception music, thinking they would fit the venue much better—and blinked even harder when they started doing a picture-perfect foxtrot together.

I glanced up at Calvin. "Am I seeing things?"

A grin lit up his face. "Not unless we're both having the same hallucination. I guess I could see why Archie might be a good dancer—didn't everyone take dance lessons back then? Cotillion, or whatever?"

It seemed Calvin had more information on that subject than I, because I'd never even heard of cotillion. But he was right—I did recall vaguely that back in the day, everyone seemed to know how to do the foxtrot, or the tango, or whatever.

You know, I would have paid serious money to see Archie perform a tango with Victoria.

But it seemed they were going to be content with just the foxtrot for now, because after the dance was over, the two of them walked over to one of the waiters who was circulating with trays of champagne, and they each plucked a glass while continuing their conversation. No sign of him being tongue-tied or shy around my wedding planner, that was for sure, but then again, I guessed that wasn't his first glass of champagne, either.

And when she excused herself after a while and walked over to check and make sure there was plenty of cake cut for anyone who still wanted a piece, I made sure to head in her direction.

"Oh, Selena," she said, looking vaguely guilty about the half-drunk glass of champagne in her hand. "I was just—"

"It's fine," I cut in. "If anyone's earned the right to let their hair down and relax a little, it's you." I stopped there, and looked past her to where Archie had sat down at the table he'd shared with some of Calvin's cousins. "Where in the world did you learn to dance like that?"

A little blush colored her cheeks, one I guessed didn't have much to do with the dance that had ended a few minutes earlier. "Oh, that," she said in deprecating tones that wouldn't have fooled anyone, even someone as tipsy as I was right then. "I just figured with planning all these weddings, it couldn't hurt to have some firsthand knowledge. It's definitely helped with coaching couples who don't want to trip over each other during their first dance but who also don't want to go to the trouble of taking real dance lessons."

That made some sense. Calvin and I weren't exactly what you could call the world's best dancers, but we'd chosen a slow, easy song for our first dance and hadn't made a hash of it. But not stepping on each other's feet wasn't exactly the same as twirling through the graceful maneuvers Victoria and Archie had just performed.

"Well, you and Archie looked great out there."

If anything, Victoria reddened even further. "He's really a marvelous dancer. I don't think I've ever met anyone who could dance like that—I mean, outside of a professional." A pause, and then she asked, "Do you know where he learned to dance?"

I shook my head. "No…I didn't even know he could. One of his little secrets, I guess. You'll have to ask him."

Once again, she was silent for a few seconds. "Maybe I will."

A smile, and she was off, threading through

the crowd on her way back to him. The smile he sent her as she approached him told me everything I wanted to know.

This reception signaled a new beginning for Calvin and me...but I thought it might be the start of something new for Archie and Victoria, too.

Only time would tell, I supposed.

Epilogue

"See you back at our house," Calvin said, and I leaned in through the open window of his SUV and gave him a hearty kiss.

"I shouldn't be too long," I told him, and he sent me a dazzling smile.

"I'll be waiting."

Another kiss, and then he rolled up the window to preserve the precious A/C on this blazing hot day before backing out of the parking space behind the building that housed my apartment and my shop.

Well, I supposed I couldn't call it "my" apartment anymore, not now that I was officially moved in with Calvin. We'd spent most of the day shuttling my personal belongings over to the sprawling adobe house we now shared, and my former home was starting to feel a little forlorn.

One last task, though…one I'd told Calvin I wanted to do on my own.

I headed back inside, glad for the rush of cool air conditioning that surrounded me. The day of our wedding had been warm but not hot, a true blessing, but full summer had descended during our ten days in Napa. Like everyone else in Arizona, I was hoping for an early monsoon season, although at the moment, there didn't seem to be much chance of one materializing any time soon.

The apartment didn't look all that different, since I wasn't moving any of the furniture to my new home. True, some photos and favorite works of art had already made the trip over in the back of Calvin's SUV, along with most of my pots and pans and kitchen utensils, but still, anyone walking in right now would probably have had a hard time figuring out that the place was unoccupied.

I passed the bedroom; my clothes and shoes and other personal items were the first things we'd transferred over to the house, so there was no reason to stop there. And even in the office, the bookshelves and walls were bare, thanks to my new husband helping me take everything down and pack it up.

All except the altar, that is.

It was such an intensely personal space that I'd

told him I wanted to do this part of the packing by myself, to carefully wrap each crystal and candle holder and pack it away, and transport it over in the back seat of my Beetle—a car I'd promised to Archie, since Calvin and I had both agreed that I really needed to buy something with four-wheel-drive so he wouldn't worry about me commuting back and forth to the store no matter what the weather conditions might be.

And although he'd been extremely vague about how he was managing to pull off such a feat, Calvin was also working on getting Archie a full set of new records—driver's license, birth certificate, high school and college diplomas—so he'd be able to reenter society with no one the wiser about all those decades he'd spent trapped in a cat's body. Apparently, this sort of process took a while, although Calvin had hinted that all the paperwork should be ready by the end of the week.

A good thing, since I knew it was important for Archie to feel as independent as possible, as though he was a part of this new century. True, he had Travis Cox, the Uber driver, to chauffeur him around, but that wasn't the same thing as having your own car. I got the impression that a good bit of Archie's impatience to get behind the wheel was due to his inability to visit Victoria; it sounded as though they'd talked on the phone more than once while I was out of town, but she was still in the thick of June wedding season and just didn't have the time to come out to Globe to see him.

From anyone else, this might have seemed like a blow-off, but I'd seen the way she'd looked at him during the reception and knew she wasn't stalling simply because she couldn't think of a tactful way to tell him she wasn't interested. No, she was just crazy-busy, and I had no doubt she would make time to go out for dinner or whatever if he could drive himself to Scottsdale instead of expecting her to travel for an hour and a half each way to see him.

A new roll of bubble wrap awaited me in the office, and I started tearing off pieces, taking my time wrapping each crystal and pendulum and candle holder, thanking each one of them for the service they'd provided me and promising them that they would be just as happy in their new home. Actually, I thought we would all be happier there—I'd gotten one of the spare bedrooms as an office, and Calvin had moved in a lovely old oak table for me to use as an altar. The room was located at the rear of the house and looked out on the beautiful wild land that surrounded the property on all sides, with mesquite and juniper and scrub oaks, and some really gorgeous rock formations. At once, I'd sensed the spot had some crazy-good energy, and so I was looking forward to working on my manifestations there.

First, though, I needed to get all this packed up. Because the crystal ball wasn't really part of my altar, it had already been moved and was now waiting in a box at my new house.

I had to hope Grandma Ellen wouldn't be too upset about being stuck in a box for a few hours. Then again, it wasn't as though she actually lived in the crystal ball, but only appeared there when I reached out to her for help.

Wrapping crystals was a tedious process. I'd added to my collection during my time here in Globe—I'd picked up some really fabulous specimens during Calvin's and my trip to Sedona and the Verde Valley the previous autumn—and so the process took longer than I'd thought. Eventually, though, everything had been transferred to the boxes he'd left in the office for me, although I was very glad we'd decided to bring extras over just to be safe.

Lugging all that stuff downstairs wasn't the most fun job in the world, although I told myself it was better to be carrying it down rather than bringing it up. And eventually, everything was stowed in the luggage compartment and in the back seat of my Beetle, ready to be transported to its new home.

I still needed to walk through the place and

make sure I hadn't missed anything, though. True, I'd be back at the store the next morning, and it wasn't as if I couldn't grab something I'd inadvertently left behind. Even so, I knew I needed to do this, my own little ritual to say goodbye to this portion of my life so I could look forward to the next.

So many memories greeted me as I paused in the living room and looked over at the window where Archie had meowed to be let in, now more than a year ago. I'd promised him that I would help him break free of the curse, but in the end, he was the only person with the power to do such a thing. Now, just like me, he had the chance to move on to a new life and new possibilities.

As far as I could tell, I hadn't overlooked anything important in my former home. I'd been a little afraid the apartment might reproach me for leaving it behind, but all I could sense was a sort of peaceful silence. While I still didn't know exactly what I wanted to do with the space, I got the feeling it would be on board with whatever I decided. Like the rest of us, it was ready to move on.

I went into the dining room and picked up my purse, then ran a hand over the dining room table. It was here that Calvin had proposed to me, where we'd shared so many happy meals.

No need to get sentimental, though—we'd

shared just as many wonderful meals at the lovely adobe house that was now mine as well, and we'd get to share thousands more. This dining room had provided what I needed at the time, but it was all right to let it go.

After engaging the alarm system, I hurriedly locked the front door before my thirty seconds of grace time was up, and then headed downstairs. While part of me wanted to peek into the store, I knew there was no need for that—I'd already planned to come in a little early the next morning so I could dust and do some tidying up before I opened for the day.

Just as I was approaching my car, I thought I saw a little scurry of movement underneath it.

A piece of paper or a plastic bag blown by the wind, or something else?

I opened the car door so I could deposit my purse on the passenger seat, then bent down to look underneath the car.

No, that definitely wasn't a plastic bag. A pair of bright little eyes stared back at me from a furry black face.

"Hey, there," I said softly. "Want to come out?"

She was a little thing, obviously a chihuahua mix of some sort. Her feathery tail gave the faintest of wags, as if she wanted to come to me but wasn't sure whether that was really the right move.

"It's okay," I told her in my gentlest, most coaxing voice. "I'm not going to hurt you."

And I sat and waited. I didn't know much about dogs, and the June heat was already making sweat trickle down my back despite the shade from the metal carport Brett had set up for me months earlier, but I knew I wasn't going to budge from that spot until the little stray came over to me.

A minute or two ticked by, but eventually she got up from where she'd been crouching by the front passenger-side wheel and tiptoed toward me. I stretched out my hands, and she jumped into my arms.

"Who are you, baby girl?" I asked, since it had felt obvious to me from the beginning that she was female. No sign of tags or a collar, but maybe she was microchipped. I wouldn't be able to find out right away, since it was a Sunday and Globe's one and only vet wasn't open.

The little dog seemed healthy, but thin. Her ears were oversized, almost bat-like, and with her white chest and delicate paws and waving flag of a tail, I thought she was one of the cutest creatures I'd ever seen.

Even if it turned out she belonged to some-one, I couldn't leave her here. No, I'd stop at the

Super Walmart and grab her some food…
although I had a feeling she'd probably be more
interested in the tri-tip Calvin was planning to
grill for dinner that night.

"Want to come home with me?" I asked, and
the dog's tail wagged again.

That seemed to settle it. I moved my purse
into the footwell, and then gently set the little
stray down on the passenger seat. She seemed to
know all about cars, because she immediately
stood up on her hind legs so she could look out
the window.

"Might want to be careful when I go around a
corner," I warned her, although that gentle admonition only got me another tail wag.

Smiling, I fastened my seatbelt, started the
engine, and backed out. The whole time, the dog
stayed on her hind legs, watching with interest as
we pulled out onto the highway, heading east.

Heading home.

Well, I'd told Calvin I wanted a dog, and it
sure looked as though the universe had provided
one for me. I'd see if she was microchipped, and
put out notices in local lost pets forums on Facebook and do whatever I could to find her family,
but my sixth sense told me none of that would
make a difference.

She'd stay with Calvin and me…and together,
we'd start a new family.

Is this the end of Selena's adventures…or not? Stay tuned to my blog and my Facebook page to find out!

And in the meantime, check out my new Lattes and Levitation cozy paranormal mystery series!

Also by Christine Pope

LATTES AND LEVITATION

(Cozy mystery/Paranormal romance)

Caffeine Before Curses (August 2022)

Muffins After Magic (October 2022)

Pastries and Prophecies (February 2023)

———

UNEXPECTED MAGIC

(Urban fantasy/Paranormal romance)

Found Objects

Finders, Keepers (July 2022)

Lost and Found (September 2022)

Finding Destiny (January 2023)

———

HEDGEWITCH FOR HIRE

(Mystery/Paranormal romance)

Grave Mistake

Social Medium

Household Demons

Perpetual Potion

Jingle Spells

Wandering Monsters

Uninvited Ghosts (July 2022)

THE WITCHES OF WHEELER PARK*

(Paranormal romance)

Storm Born

Thunder Road

Winds of Change

Mind Games

A Wheeler Park Christmas

Blood Ties

Healing Hands

Wishful Thinking

Smoke and Mirrors

MISS PRIMM'S ACADEMY FOR WAYWARD
WITCHES*

(Fantasy/Academy Romance)

Misspelled

THE WITCHES OF CANYON ROAD*

(Paranormal Romance)

Hidden Gifts

Darker Paths

Mysterious Ways

A Canyon Road Christmas

Demon Born

An Ill Wind

Higher Ground

Haunted Hearts

THE WITCHES OF CLEOPATRA HILL*

(Paranormal Romance)

Darkangel

Darknight

Darkmoon

Sympathetic Magic

Protector

Spellbound

A Cleopatra Hill Christmas

Impractical Magic

Strange Magic

The Arrangement

Defender

Bad Blood

Deep Magic

Darktide

THE DJINN WARS*

(Paranormal Romance)

Chosen

Taken

Fallen

Broken

Forsaken

Forbidden

Awoken

Illuminated

Stolen

Forgotten

Driven

Unspoken

THE WATCHERS TRILOGY*

(Paranormal Romance)

Falling Dark

Dead of Night

Rising Dawn

THE SEDONA FILES*

(Paranormal Romance)

Bad Vibrations

Desert Hearts

Angel Fire

Star Crossed

Falling Angels

Enemy Mine

TALES OF THE LATTER KINGDOMS*

(Fantasy Romance)

All Fall Down

Dragon Rose

Binding Spell

Ashes of Roses

One Thousand Nights

Threads of Gold

The Wolf of Harrow Hall

Moon Dance

The Song of the Thrush

THE GAIAN CONSORTIUM SERIES*

(Science Fiction Romance)

Beast (free prequel novella)

Blood Will Tell

Breath of Life

The Gaia Gambit

The Mandala Maneuver

The Titan Trap

The Zhore Deception

The Refugee Ruse

STANDALONE TITLES

Hearts on Fire

Taking Dictation

Golden Heart

Night Music: A Modern Reimagining of The Phantom of the Opera

Ghost Dance: A Sequel to Gaston Leroux's The Phantom of the Opera

Flight Before Christmas

* Indicates a completed series

About the Author

USA Today bestselling author Christine Pope has been writing stories ever since she commandeered her family's Smith-Corona typewriter back in grade school. Her work includes paranormal romance, cozy paranormal mystery, and urban fantasy, among others. She makes her home in New Mexico.

Don't miss out on any of Christine's new releases —sign up for her newsletter today!

Christine Pope on the Web:
www.christinepope.com